"We can't have a relationship."

Shelley stood her ground. "It wouldn't be right."

"It feels pretty good to me," argued Ben as he imprisoned her between the wall and his taut body. "When are you going to stop pretending it's any different for you?"

"It is different for me," Shelley lied. "Ben, I think you should know, my relationship with my boss isn't over." She ached to give in to the hungry demands his nearness was making upon her. "I...just needed a breathing space. And...this holiday provided it."

"Are you telling me it was as good with him as it is with us?"

Shelley hesitated. He'd inadvertently given her the means of his own destruction. She had only to say yes, and their tenuous relationship would be over....

Books by Anne Mather

STORMSPELL
WILD CONCERTO
HIDDEN IN THE FLAME

HARLEQUIN PRESENTS

HARLEQUIN ROMANCE

ANNE MATHER

stolen summer

Harlequin Books

TORONTO • NEW YORK • LONDON
AMSTERDAM • PARIS • SYDNEY • HAMBURG
STOCKHOLM • ATHENS • TOKYO • MILAN

Harlequin Presents first edition December 1985
ISBN 0-373-10843-5

Original hardcover edition published in 1985
by Mills & Boon Limited

CHAPTER ONE

IT was a little after four o'clock when Shelley reached the turn-off Marsha had indicated in her letter. 'Just a few miles beyond the Ripon roundabout,' she had written. 'Just look for the sign for Bedale and Leyburn. It's the A684. You can't miss it!'

And she hadn't, reflected Shelley thankfully, glad there was only about an hour of her journey left. In spite of the high speeds she had been able to maintain on the motorway, she was tired, and she half wished she had taken Marsha's advice and come up by train instead.

But at least this way she would have a car to use while she was here, Shelley reminded herself firmly. And she might be glad of that, bearing in mind Marsha's own description of the area in which she lived. Craygill was not served by buses, and there were no convenient underground stations within walking distance of her home. Indeed, Shelley had always been amazed that her friend had adapted herself to life in a Yorkshire dale so easily, after spending the first thirty-eight years of her existence in London. But, evidently, Marsha liked it. Her letters were always full of the enjoyment she got from working in such picturesque surroundings, and the infrequent visits she had made back to the capital had never tempted her to remain.

And ever since she had decided to go and live in the area, to be near her son, Marsha had been trying to persuade Shelley to come and visit. 'You're like everyone else,' she exclaimed. 'You think there's nothing worth seeing north of Watford!' she declared, completely forgetting that Shelley had been born and bred in Teesdale, and had lived there for the first six years of her life.

Not that Shelley could remember those early years too well. Her father, the younger son of a farming family, disappointed all his relatives by showing more interest in books and learning than in how many ewes his father was breeding. Nevertheless, he stuck in at school and eventually gained a place in a university, returning home at twenty-two to teach in the local school. But there were changes being made. Small schools were being closed and the pupils bussed to larger establishments. Shelley's father, married by this time and responsible for a family, found himself out of a job, and rather than accept his parent's charity, he had moved south, to Hampshire, and resumed his teaching career.

The only time afterwards that Shelley remembered visiting the farm at Tarnside was when she was twelve, and her grandfather died. Her parents went north for the funeral, but it had not been a comfortable occasion. Her father's elder brother, Uncle George, seemed to imagine the only reason they had come was to stake some claim to the farm, that he had worked for since he was a boy. There had been a lot of unpleasantness after the funeral was over, and although her grandmother had tried to adjudicate between the two brothers, they had not parted on the best of terms. Neither Shelley, nor her parents, had gone back to Tarnside, and these days Shelley had no idea if her uncle was even still alive. Her own parents were dead, killed in an avalanche during a ski-ing holiday in Austria, just after she had started working for the *Courier*.

It had been a crushing blow to the twenty-one-year-old Shelley, particularly as she had been a much-loved only child. But it was a blessing that because of her job with the London daily newspaper she was no longer living at home. After a tearful weekend, going through the rooms which held so many happy memories, she put sentiment aside and sold the house, using the money to move out of the bed-sitter—which had been all she could afford—and into a flat of her own. It had been a painful business, but at least that way she was able to keep some of her most treasured possessions; and the furniture in her bedroom, and the chesterfield, where her mother used to sit and sew, were a constant reminder of her childhood.

Of course, that was all in the past now, Shelley mused reminiscently, as she drove through Aiskew into Bedale, and admired the blue face of the church clock that looked down over the High Street. 'Four-fifteen,' she murmured, resisting the temptation to stop for some refreshment. Marsha had said she would have tea waiting for her, and it wouldn't be fair to waste time so close to her destination.

Marsha! A faint smile touched her lips as she thought about the woman who had brought her to this enchanting part of England. And it was enchanting, with its sun-dappled fields and blossom-covered hedges, all burgeoning now as spring gave way to early summer. She had not expected it to be quite so civilised, after her recollections of Teesdale, but the countryside around the little market town was infinitely pleasing. Crakehall; Patrick Brompton; even the names were delightful. She was so grateful to Marsha for inviting her. It was exactly the sort of change she needed. Once again, Marsha had come to her rescue, and she looked forward to the day when she could repay her in some way.

She had first met Marsha just a few weeks after her parents were killed. Marsha had stormed into the office to complain about an article one of the *Courier's* correspondents had written about her, and because it was February and many of the staff had succumbed to the current 'flu epidemic, Shelley had been asked to deal with her.

In fact, the interview had not turned out at all as she had anticipated. Having heard of Marsha Manning, having admired her work for some time, Shelley was able to understand the painter's anger at being patronised, at being called an *artist*, and at being described as a lonely woman, taking out her frustration in oils and canvas. The fact that Marsha's marriage had broken up only months before the article was written had fuelled the reporter's penchant for drama, and what had begun as a serious discussion of Marsha's work had deteriorated into little more than a libellous attack on her private life.

From the start, Shelley had sympathised with the other woman, and although there was more than ten years difference in their ages, and Marsha was much more worldly-wise and cynical, nevertheless, a curious friendship had grown up between them. It was a friendship strengthened by their mutual sense of loss—Shelley had missed her parents dreadfully in those early days, and Marsha was still recovering from a rather messy divorce. A casual invitation to lunch had initiated an association that had become one of the most important elements in Shelley's life, and the years since then had only fortified the affection they had for one another.

In a way, Shelley admitted, Marsha had taken

the place of her parents. Not as a mother; she was too young for that; but perhaps as an understanding older sister, someone Shelley could turn to for advice about the things—and people—that were important to her. She had grown used to turning up at Marsha's studio at all hours of the day and night, knowing she was always welcome. They might not always talk; sometimes, when Marsha was engrossed in her work, Shelley would just sit and watch her; but she was there, she cared, and that was what was important. Naturally, Marsha had been the recipient of many confidences, not least those of a personal nature. As well as a willing ear, she offered a shoulder to cry on, something Shelley had been grateful for when her problems got too tough.

Of course, Shelley was working in a tough profession, that became tougher still when she left the *Courier* and joined the staff of Capitol Television. As a very junior associate-producer she had to suffer a lot of back-biting and jealousy, particularly when it became known that the station manager, Mike Berlitz, had a more than professional interest in her career.

In the meantime, Marsha's career flourished. Her paintings—impressionist landscapes mostly—were proving popular with critics, and she was invited to show a collection of her work at the Shultz Gallery, a very singular honour indeed. Her son, who was away at school, returned home for his mother's exhibition, and Shelley attended the opening with them, proud to be a part of Marsha's well-deserved success.

It had been a less pleasant surprise when, four years ago, Marsha had decided to move to Wensleydale. With the success of her work, and the fact that she had nothing to keep her in

London, she had decided to move north to be near
her son, who had left university now, and joined a
veterinary practice there. 'Shades of James
Herriot,' she had said ruefully, smiling at Shelley's
shocked expression. 'Darling, don't look like that.
Craygill is not the end of the earth. It's just a
couple of hundred miles up the motorway, with a
magical mystery tour at the end of it.'

But Shelley had been less enthusiastic. Her work
was demanding, and she seldom had time for
holidays. Besides, the idea of driving hundreds of
miles just to spend a few days in rural
surroundings had seemed too much trouble, and
although she and Marsha spoke together often
over the 'phone, their meetings had been confined
to Marsha's visits to London.

Until now, Shelley acknowledged wearily, the
ache behind her eyes becoming an actual physical
strain. It would have been easier if the winding
country roads had been at the start of her journey,
she conceded. Right now, even the undoubted
beauty of her surroundings was little compensation. She wanted to get to her destination, take a
hot bath, and go to bed. Marsha would
understand. Marsha always had. That was why
she had invited her.

The signs for Leyburn brought her into a busy
market place, where several roads converged. Not
much further now, she told herself encouragingly,
turning her sleek little sports saloon on to the road
for Aysgarth. Fifteen miles, at the most. With a bit
of luck she'd be there soon after five o'clock.

As luck would have it, the roads were not busy
once she left the town behind. But the constant
convolutions of the route made any relaxation
impossible, and she felt the sweat break out on her
forehead as the throbbing in her head increased.

And then, without warning, the fanbelt snapped. One minute she was driving smoothly along a cathedral-like avenue of trees, and the next she heard the distinctive clatter as the rubber tore free of its housing, leaving her without any means to cool her already heated engine.

'Damn, damn, *damn*!'

With a exclamation of disgust, Shelley drew the Ford into the side of the road and switched off the ignition. She had passed a village a couple of miles back, but she didn't remember seeing a garage there. In any case, the idea of setting out to walk for any distance with an aching back and a throbbing head did not bear thinking about, and she decided she would have to wait until another car came by.

Pushing open her door, she got out, stretching her long slim body with real relief. As a matter of fact, she felt better out of the stuffy confines of the car. Leaning against the bonnet, she tipped back her head and let the cooling air blow refreshingly over her shoulders and sighed. Perhaps she should have taken a break, after all, she reflected. The fanbelt just might have lasted, if she hadn't sustained the pressure.

The sound of a car's engine caused her to take notice, but the shabby estate car, driven by a woman, swept by without pause. Oh, well, thought Shelley resignedly, it was going in the wrong direction anyway. Another vehicle would be along shortly. And this time she'd make sure the driver saw her.

But, in fact, several cars passed her without stopping; tourists, she suspected, with wives and children who regarded Shelley with unconcealed curiosity. Perhaps her appearance put them off, she thought uneasily. She was so accustomed to

the kinks and mores of London society, she had
seen nothing unusual in the very masculine lines of
her black Edwardian-style pants suit, but here,
miles from her normal habitat, she did feel slightly
out of place. The tawny-red brilliance of her hair
fought a losing battle with the loose peacock blue
shirt that fell open at her throat, and although it
had been neat when she left her flat that morning,
by now her agitation had made a bird's nest of its
knot.

There was nothing else for it, she reflected
wearily. She would have to walk, after all. At least,
to the nearest' phone box. Perhaps if she could
reach Marsha, she would come out and pick her
up. They could arrange for the car to be dealt with
later.

Her spirits marginally less bleak, Shelley
collected her bulky shoulder bag from the back of
the car and locked the doors. Then, with a
determined expellation of air from her lungs, she
set off, not deigning to lift her thumb, even when a
dust-smeared Land-Rover accelerated past her.
Thank heavens it's not raining, she thought,
glancing down at the expensive suede boots which
encased her legs to the knee. She had not expected
to go hiking, and their velvety exterior would soon
have been spoiled by trudging through muddy
water. She supposed she should be 'thankful for
small mercies', as her mother used to say. It would
not hurt her to get some exercise. Even if the
doctor had warned her not to subject herself to
any stress, he meant stress of a different kind. Not
the simple aggravation aroused at being forced to
use her legs.

It was a few seconds before she realised the
Land-Rover that had passed her had stopped up
ahead. She had been involved with her own

problems, and she had not noticed the stationary vehicle. But now, as she approached, the driver got out and walked round the back of the automobile to meet her, his expression half amused as he took in her appearance.

He was a young man, in his mid-twenties, she estimated, with dark blond hair, combed smoothly from a side parting. He was tall and lean and muscular, with hard tanned features and good bone structure. He was not conventionally hand-some. The contours of his face were too irregular for that. But he was very attractive, with a thin-lipped mouth and heavily-lidded eyes, that were somehow oddly familiar.

Gathering her self-possession, Shelley gave him her most scintillating smile. If he was about to offer her a lift, she was not going to refuse it, even if she was a little chary about accepting help from a solitary stranger. She would have preferred to get assistance from one of those men who had had their wives sitting beside them, but they had not offered it. Besides, after living in London for almost ten years, she felt reasonably capable of handling any situation, and younger men, with ambitions, could usually be crushed by her intellect.

'You couldn't tell me where I might find a garage, could you?' she enquired now, before he could speak. 'I've broken the fanbelt on my car, and I'm a stranger to the area.'

'Yes?' The humour in the man's expression deepened, and Shelley felt a rising sense of irritation. She was more accustomed to being the object of male admiration, rather than a source of amusement, and he had far too much self-confidence for someone of his age.

'Yes,' she replied, a little tersely, running an

annoyingly nervous hand around the back of her neck. 'You probably saw my car a few yards back. A red XR3, with black lines along the side.'

'I saw it,' he agreed, and apparently making a sterling effort to control his levity, he gestured towards his own vehicle. 'Get in. I'll give you a lift to Low Burton. There's a garage there, that can probably help you. If not, I may be able to take you wherever you want to go.'

Shelley hesitated. 'How far is Low Burton?'

The man shrugged. 'About half a mile.'

'So near?'

'Well—maybe three-quarters,' he conceded carelessly. 'But it's quite a climb—unless you're used to it, of course.'

Shelley looked at him sharply, detecting criticism in his words, but there was no mockery in his expression now. On the contrary, he had pushed his hands into the waistline pockets of his tight-fitting jeans and was regarding her with a certain amount of sympathy—an intent appraisal that Shelley, in spite of her resentment, found disturbingly mature.

'And—you think this garage may have what I need?' she asked stiffly, feeling at a disadvantage and not liking it.

'I should think so.' The man inclined his head. 'We have grass track racing in these parts occasionally, and Jack Smedley gets a lot of business that way. I shouldn't think a broken fanbelt will present too many problems to him.'

'Oh—all right.' Glad for once of her five-feet nine inches which meant, with her heeled boots, that they were almost on eye-level terms, Shelley acquiesced. 'Thank you,' she added belatedly, as he closed the Land-Rover's passenger door behind her, and she heard him say drily: 'It's a pleasure!'

The Land-Rover was not a very salubrious form of transport. It smelled of what Shelley could only imagine were animals, and a glance over her shoulder essayed the information that some creature or other had been carried in the back quite recently. There was a mess of straw strewn over the floor, and distinct signs of a certain lack of continence. It made her wonder if she had not been a little premature in accepting a lift, and perhaps her erstwhile knight errant should have warned her of the disadvantages before he offered her a ride.

But it was an uncharitable notion, and she speedily dismissed it. After all, the seat she was sitting on was clean, and it was saving her an obviously arduous climb. And the young man beside her probably found nothing distasteful about good, wholesome, country scents, and he himself was perfectly presentable.

Permitting herself a brief glance in his direction, Shelley had to admit he was nothing at all like the image she had kept of her father's brother. Yet he was, apparently, a farmer—or a farmer's son. He obviously spent a lot of time out of doors, evidenced by his dark tan, which was so unusual against the lightness of his hair. And the shirt he was wearing, that was rolled back along his forearms and opened at the neck to expose the strong column of his throat, revealed the taut muscles flexing beneath his skin, skin that was lightly covered by sun-bleached hair. Her gaze dropped to his legs, long and powerful beneath the blue denim. They would be taut and muscled, too, she knew. He was probably the local heart-throb, she decided wryly, deliberately mocking her own unwilling interest. A nice boy, but definitely much too young for her, even had she been looking for diversion—which she wasn't.

Shaking her head, she looked away, but not before he had intercepted her appraisal. For a moment, her green-eyed gaze was caught and held by the silvery greyness of his. Then, feeling obliged to say something, if only to dispel her own disconcertment, Shelley found the words to break the pregnant silence.

'It's my first visit to Wensleydale,' she said, transferring her attention to the window. 'I didn't realise it was quite so pretty. Do you—live around here, Mr——'

'Seton,' he supplied evenly. 'Ben Seton. And yes. I live in Low Burton, actually.'

'You do?' Shelley looked at him again, but this time she avoided those disturbing eyes. 'So you do know the area very well indeed.'

'Well enough,' he conceded, with a faint smile, and Shelley found herself resenting his cool composure. 'Didn't you believe me?'

'Why shouldn't I?' Shelley lifted one disdainful shoulder. 'This is hardly the sort of vehicle you'd abduct anybody in!'

He grinned then, a satisfying relaxation of his features that caused an unwilling ripple of reaction to slide along Shelley's spine. 'I'm sorry,' he said, though she suspected he was nothing of the sort. 'I'm so used to this old heap, I didn't think you might object to it.'

'I don't—object to it.' Shelley made an effort to be civil. 'I'm sure it serves its purpose admirably.'

'Oh, it does.' The humour was still there in his expression. 'Though I have to admit,' he added, 'it's some time since I used the back for anything other than hauling animals!'

Shelly pressed her lips together. 'I only meant—it smells,' she said shortly, and he inclined his head.

'Not what you're used to, I'm sure,' he commented lazily, and sensitive to any scepticism, Shelley's patience snapped.

'No, it's not,' she retorted sharply. 'I'm from London, actually. I'm a television producer.' She waited for him to absorb this, and then continued less aggressively: 'So you see, riding around in muck-laden farm vehicles is hardly an everyday occurrence for me.'

'I'm sure it's not.' His response was as deferential as she could have wished, yet she still had the uneasy suspicion he was only humouring her. Did he believe her? Or did he think she was only making it up to impress him? It was infuriating to realise that she cared what he thought.

'I'm going to stay with Miss Manning at Craygill,' she appended, refusing to admit she was trying to verify her statement. 'Marsha Manning, that is. You may have heard of her. She's a paint——'

'I've heard of her,' he interrupted carelessly, cutting off her explanation. 'This is Low Burton, just ahead, by the way. Jack Smedley's place is just off the square.'

He slowed to take a particularly sharp bend and when the road straightened out again, Shelley saw the dry stone wall of a churchyard on her left. The road ran between the wall of the church and the wall of the rectory opposite, before cottages appeared on either side, their gardens bright with blossom. Shelley identified lobelia and aubretia, and showers of snow-on-the-mountain, before the cottages too gave way to narrow town houses, with leaded window panes and polished letter-boxes.

Her attention to her surroundings precluded any

further conversation, and she was relieved. She was not usually so touchy about her job, and she seldom, if ever, felt the need to brag about her importance. But this man—whoever he was—had the ability to tear away the façade she had erected around herself during the past ten years, and reduce her to the state of defending her position.

A few yards further on they entered the small market square, with a clock-tower chiming the hour, and a handful of cars parked near a group of municipal buildings. There were shops, and a small supermarket, and a collection of public houses and, just around the corner, the blue-and-white sign indicating Smedley's Garage.

'Would you like me to find out if he has what you want?' her companion asked, bringing the Land-Rover to a halt by the petrol pumps.

Shelley hesitated only a moment, and then shook her head. 'That's okay,' she said. 'I can manage,' even though she was tempted to take advantage of his offer. It would be easier for him to approach the garage owner, who he obviously knew, and explain what was required, but Shelley felt the need to demonstrate her independence. She had no intention of providing him with any more amusement. She had already proved herself to be both vain and shrewish, and no doubt his friends would enjoy his story of a helpless older woman, bowled over by his charm. Men always liked to exaggerate, and her behaviour would hardly invite his discretion.

Now, opening her bag, she searched for her wallet. 'Will you let me buy you a drink, Mr Seton,' she began, determined to restore the relationship to its proper footing, but once again he prevented her.

'That won't be necessary,' he said, a faint edge

to his voice now, as he flicked the flap of her bag back into place. Closing his fingers over the soft leather, he successfully trapped her hand inside, and his eyes were steel-hard as they met her frustrated gaze. 'Never let it be said that a dalesman couldn't offer a lady assistance, without requiring some payment for it.' Her hand struggled to be free, and he let go of the bag again. 'Enjoy your holiday,' he added, as she thrust open her door. 'Who knows—we may see one another again!'

'I should think that will be highly unlikely!' Shelley muttered under her breath, as she climbed out of the Land-Rover. And, although she didn't look back as she strode confidently into the garage, she was conscious of his eyes upon her, until she was out of sight.

CHAPTER TWO

IT was six o'clock by the time Shelley reached Craygill, and she unutterably relieved when, on the outskirts of the tiny hamlet, she found the house she was looking for. Marsha had said to look out for two stone gateposts, because the sign indicating the house was worn and scarcely readable from the driving seat of a car. But Shelley saw the crumbling notice for Askrigg House as she turned between the stone sentinels, and she accelerated up the gravelled drive, to the detriment of the car's paintwork.

Marsha appeared at the door of the rambling old building as Shelley reached the circular forecourt before the house. Dressed in paint-smeared slacks and an equally disreputable smock, she looked so endearingly familiar that Shelley could hardly wait to get out of the car to embrace her.

'Where have you been?' Marsha exclaimed fiercely, after they had exchanged their initial greetings. 'My dear, I've been practically frantic! Your daily woman said you left London at eleven o'clock this morning. I've been expecting you since four, and anticipating the worst since half-past-five!'

'Oh, love, I'm sorry!' Leaving her suitcases at Marsha's suggestion, Shelley ran a weary hand over the untidy coil of her hair as she accompanied her friend into the house. There was ivy on the walls, and honeysuckle growing over the door, but she scarcely registered her surroundings. 'It was further than I thought, and I was feeling so tired, I thought I wasn't going to make it. Then, about a dozen miles back, the fanbelt broke, and I had to—to get a lift into Low Burton, to find a garage that could fix it.'

'Smedley's, no doubt,' remarked Marsha, nodding as she led the way through a darkly panelled hall into a pleasant, airy, living room. 'Oh— Sarah!' This as a plum-cheeked girl straightened from setting a tray of tea on the low table in front of the fireplace. 'Will you collect Miss Hoyt's luggage from her car, and put it up in her room? And tell Mrs Carr we'll probably want dinner a little later than usual. Say—about eight o'clock.'

'Yes, Miss Manning.'

The girl gave Shelley a swift assessing look as she left the room. She was evidently curious about her employer's new house guest, and Marsha pulled a rueful face when Shelley arched her brows enquiringly.

'Don't mind Sarah,' she said, as soon as the door had closed behind her. She helped Shelley off with her thigh-length jacket and folded it over the back of a chair. 'If you intend to dress as a fashion model here, you'll have to get used to people staring.' She smiled to allay Shelley's protests. 'Oh, darling, it's so good to see you. Even if it could have been in happier circumstances!'

'I'm fine—really,' said Shelley, sinking down gratefully into the soft cushions of a chintz-covered armchair. 'Mmm, you've no idea how good it is to relax at last! I seem to have been travelling for days!'

'It must have been infuriating, losing the fanbelt so close to your destination,' agreed Marsha, sympathising. 'Who gave you a lift?'

'Oh—just a man,' said Shelley dismissively,

annoyed with herself for re-opening the topic. For some ridiculous reason, she was loath to discuss that particular episode at the moment, probably because Ben Seton had already occupied far too much of her time. 'What a comfortable room this is, Marsha,' she added, changing the subject. 'And what a clever idea—filling the fireplace with flowers!'

Marsha was diverted, and seating herself opposite, beside the tea tray, she became absorbed with the cups. 'Milk and sugar?' she asked. 'Or would you prefer something stronger?'

'If I have something stronger, I'll probably fall asleep,' confessed Shelley lightly. 'Honestly, tea is just what I need.'

'Good.' Marsha filled two cups and after offering Shelley a hot, buttered scone, she lay back in her chair and regarded her friend with evident satisfaction. 'You're here at last,' she said, her grey eyes warm with affection. 'And not before time. Shelley, why didn't you tell me what was going on?'

Shelley sighed, nibbling the half scone she had accepted without any real appetite. 'There was nothing to tell,' she answered flatly. 'It was just an accumulation of circumstances, and Mike's wife dying like that, seemed to bring them all to a head.'

Marsha shook her head. 'I thought you were in love with him.'

'So did I.' Shelley lifted her slim shoulders. 'But I wasn't.'

Marsha shook her head. 'You've lost weight.'

'A few pounds.' Shelley was offhand. 'I could afford it. I spend too much of my life sitting down.'

'Nevertheless . . .' Marsha finished her tea and

propped her elbows on her knees. 'The—specialist you saw would not have ordered you to take a complete rest if he hadn't considered you needed it.'

'The shrink, you mean?' prompted Shelley drily. 'Don't be afraid to say it, Marsha. I guess I got myself into quite a state, one way and another. And having Guy Livingstone on my back hasn't helped. He can't wait to step into my shoes.'

'Mice on a treadmill!' Marsha sighed. 'Shelley, don't you sometimes wonder if you were really cut out to be a career woman! I mean—don't get me wrong—but there is another life, outside your profession.'

'That! From you!' Shelley put the remains of her scone aside and looked at her friend incredulously. 'You're not exactly a walking recommendation of the eternal wife and mother!'

'I know, I know.' Marsha was not offended. 'But just because my marriage to Tom didn't work out, doesn't mean I can't appreciate the institution when it does.' She shrugged. 'I suppose, living around here, has given me a different outlook on life. Oh—I'm not saying that if Tom and I were still together, things would be any different. But he did give me Dickon, and I'm eternally grateful for that.'

'You don't have to get married to have a baby,' pointed out Shelley wryly. Then, smiling, she added: 'How is Dickon anyway? I'm looking forward to meeting him again.'

'And he's keen to meet you,' declared Marsha eagerly. 'Do you remember when we all went to that exhibition of mine at the Shultz Gallery? He talked about you for days afterwards. I think he had quite a crush on you!'

Shelley laughed. It was the first time she had

really relaxed for months, and it was so good to anticipate the weeks ahead, with nothing more arduous to occupy her mind than how she was going to fill her days.

'He's engaged now,' Marsha continued reflectively, her thoughts evidently still with her son. 'She's a nice girl. Her name is Jennifer Chater. She's the daughter of one of his partners in the practice.'

'The veterinary practice,' said Shelley nodding. 'When will he be home?'

'Oh, Dickon doesn't live here,' said Marsha quickly. 'In winter, we often get snowed in, and he has to be available for calls. He bought a house in Low Burton, just after he joined Langley and Chater.'

'Low Burton,' echoed Shelley faintly, wondering if she would ever hear the name without thinking of Ben Seton. 'And—will he and Jennifer live there, after they're married?'

'Initially, perhaps,' agreed Marsha doubtfully. 'But it's not very big. Not big enough for a family,' she added, her eyes twinkling. 'I can't wait to become a grandmother! But I don't suppose I have any choice.'

'Are they getting married soon?' asked Shelley, willing to talk about anything that would not remind her of the young man in the Land-Rover, and Marsha shrugged.

'Provisionally the date is set for sometime in October,' she replied. 'But it really depends on Jennifer's father. He hasn't been at all well lately, and consequently Dickon thinks they ought to wait and see what happens.'

'I see.' Shelley sighed. 'Is he coming over this evening?'

'He was, but now he's not.' Marsha sounded

regretful, but Shelley couldn't deny a sudden feeling of relief. Although she didn't feel nearly as exhausted now as she had earlier, she was glad there was only to be the two of them for dinner. 'As a matter of fact, he rang, just before you arrived,' Marsha added. 'I thought it might be you, but of course, it wasn't. He had intended to join us for dinner, but something's come up. He said to give you his regards, and that he'll probably see us tomorrow.'

In spite of being tired, Shelley did not sleep as well as she had expected. She and Marsha had enjoyed a leisurely dinner, served by Marsha's housekeeper, Mrs Carr, and then adjourned to the living room to continue their conversation over a nightcap. The brandy, plus the half bottle of wine she had consumed, should have assured her of a decent night's rest, but once her head touched the pillow, Shelley's brain sprang into action. No matter how determinedly she endeavoured to relax, the events of the day persistently disturbed her rest, and the absence of any sounds but the wind through the beech trees at the bottom of Marsha's garden and the occasional cry of an owl, accentuated the strangeness of her surroundings. She was used to the sound of traffic, to the constant hum of a city that never sleeps. Here the stillness was almost deafening, and every creak of the old house was magnified a dozen times.

She eventually got up and took a sleeping pill, just as the birds were beginning their dawn chorus. She supposed it was around four, but she was too weary to pay much attention to the time. She crawled back under the feather duvet and lost consciousness almost immediately, only to wake with a dry mouth and an aching head, when someone pulled back the flowered curtains.

It was Sarah, Shelley saw through slitted lids, and she thought how appropriate it was that the girl should be the one to see her like this. Struggling up against her pillows, she was instantly aware of how haggard she must look without make-up, and with the vivid tangle of her hair loose about her shoulders. No fashion model now, she acknowledged drily, as Sarah's sharp eyes took in her appearance. Just a rather worn-looking woman, stripped of the protection her sophistication had given her.

'Good morning, miss.' Sarah left the window to come back to the bed, and now Shelley noticed the tray of tea the girl had set on the table beside her.

'Good morning,' she responded, pulling up the strap of her nightgown, which had fallen over one shoulder, and trying to ignore the painful throbbing of her head. 'What time is it?'

'Eight-thirty, miss,' answered Sarah at once, seemingly enjoying the reversal of their positions. She lifted the tray and set it across Shelley's legs. 'Shall I pour this for you, or can you manage it yourself?'

'I think I can do it,' murmured Shelley evenly, refusing to be drawn by the girl's pertness. And, as Sarah tossed her head carelessly, and marched towards the door, Marsha herself put her head around it.

'Oh, you are awake!' she exclaimed, coming into the room as the maid departed, revealing she was still in her dressing gown. 'I asked Mrs Carr to send you up some tea, just in case you were awake. But, as you are, perhaps you'd like breakfast as well.'

'Oh, no.' Shelley put the tray of tea aside and threaded long slim fingers through her hair. She refrained from mentioning that she hadn't been awake until Sarah chose to disturb her. If it was half-past-eight, it was late enough. 'Honestly, Marsha, I'm not an invalid. And I'm not going to spend my holiday lying in bed. I'll come downstairs and have some coffee and toast, if I may. Just give me fifteen minutes to take a shower and put some clothes on.'

'Don't bother to dress!' Marsha waved a dismissing hand. 'My dear, there's only the two of us, and I rarely put my clothes on before ten o'clock—unless I'm feeling very virtuous, which isn't often.' She smiled. 'Mrs Carr sets the table in the morning room, and I usually spend an hour or so going over the papers. I get half a dozen delivered. It's the only way to keep up to date with the news.'

'All right.' Shelley was not prepared to argue. As soon as Marsha had gone, she intended to take a couple of headache capsules, and it would be rather pleasant just to take things easy for once.

'Good.' Marsha was pleased. 'Well, I'll leave you to wash your hands.' Her eyes twinkled. 'See you downstairs in five minutes.'

After her friend had gone, Shelley slid out of bed and padded across to the window. She had left her bag on the window seat, and she perched there as she rummaged for the small carton that contained the paracetamol capsules. Swallowing two, she looked out of the window, thinking how ironic it was that even in these idyllic surroundings she was still a prey to her nerves. But it would pass, she told herself firmly. The psychiatrist had said that all she needed was a complete rest, away from the petty jealousies she had never really learned to live with, and away from Mike, whose emotional blackmail simply wasn't going to work.

After rinsing her face and cleaning her teeth in

the bathroom, Shelley picked up her kimono-style wrapper from the end of the bed, and slid her arms into the sleeves. Made of jade-green satin and appliquéd with white flowers around the wide sleeves and the hem, it was her favourite robe, not least because Marsha herself had bought it for her in Tokyo almost five years ago.

A brief appraisal of her appearance necessitated that she take a brush to her hair, and she grimaced at her reflection as the thick coarse strands resisted her efforts. She had often been tempted to have her hair cut, but although she had it trimmed from time to time, it still hung well below her shoulders. Usually, she wore it in a loose coil at the nape of her neck or occasionally, as the day before, she wound it into a knot on top of her head, which made her look even taller.

Abandoning the task, she pushed heelless mules on to her feet, and opened her door. Marsha had briefly explained the lay-out of the house to her the night before, and Shelley easily made her way to the head of the stairs, and descended slowly. The balustrade was smooth, after years of use and Mrs Carr's polishing, and a warm red carpet underfoot gave colour to the panelled wall that mounted beside her. Some of Marsha's paintings had been hung to provide their own illumination, and someone had filled a copper urn with armfuls of white and purple lilac, that scented the air with its perfume.

Downstairs, she found the morning room easily. The door was standing ajar, and she could see a round table spread with a white tablecloth and smell the delicious aroma of coffee. Marsha had evidently gone to tell Mrs Carr that her guest would not be requiring breakfast in bed, and Shelley entered the room without hesitation, halting abruptly at the sight of a man, lounging at the side of the table which had been hidden from the door. He had a newspaper propped in front of him, and all Shelley could initially see was one leg, encased in cream denim, the foot resting carelessly on the leg of the chair beside him, and one arm, which revealed he was wearing a matching denim shirt. The sleeve of his shirt was rolled back almost to his elbow, exposing a lean brown arm, and his wrist was encircled by a slim gold watch which, in spite of its leather strap, looked rather exclusive. It was the sort of present Marsha would buy, Shelley suspected, guessing who it must be. But she was unwilling to face anyone else in her present state of undress, and she would have withdrawn unseen had he not chosen that moment to lower the newspaper.

'*You!*'

Shelley's instinctive embarrassment at being caught out gave way to blank astonishment at the sight of the man, who was now withdrawing his foot from its resting place and getting to his feet. It was the man from the Land-Rover—Ben Seton— and for several seconds she forgot her appearance in the numbness of disbelief.

'Good morning, Miss Hoyt—or can I call you Shelley?' he enquired, evidently deriving as much amusement from her reaction today as he had from her frustration the day before, and Shelley fought to regain her sense of balance. What was he doing here? she asked herself abstractedly. How had he found her? And how did he know her name, when she herself hadn't told him. Marsha! she thought intuitively. Marsha must know he was here. And with that awareness, came another sickening realisation . . .

As if her sudden, dawning knowledge was

written in her eyes for him to read, he put the newspaper aside, and came easily across the room to stand in front of her. Without her heels, he seemed much taller than he had done the day before, and she knew an ominous feeling of presentiment when he put his hands upon her shoulders.

'I'm sorry,' he said, and she knew now why his eyes had briefly seemed so familiar. 'I know I should have told you yesterday, but when you didn't recognise me, I decided you deserved all you got.' His lips tilted, and his teeth were very white against his dark skin. 'I was going to come over last evening for dinner, but I took pity on you, after all. I guessed—after the day you had had— you might not be able to stand any more shocks.'

Shelley didn't know which emotion she felt strongest—anger, at his deliberate deception; resentment, that he should still be treating her with the same mixture of good humour and tolerance he had displayed the day before; or *panic*, at the fact he had come back into her life and overthrown her resolution not to think of him again.

'Are you angry with me?' he asked softly, and aware that Marsha could come upon them at any time, and she was in no state to deal with *that*, Shelley gave a helpless shake of her head.

'I—why—you were only about seventeen, when I saw you last,' she stammered, looking up at him and then wishing she hadn't. He really had the most fantastic eyes, dark grey at the moment, and fringed with thick silvery lashes, that accentuated their beauty. A person could drown in those eyes, she thought unwillingly, unable to drag her gaze away, until his tightening fingers on her shoulders brought her quickly to her senses. 'W-where is your mother?'

'In the kitchen,' said Marsha's son flatly, allowing her to step back from his hands, and Shelley, reminded of her unwelcome state of undress, wrapped the folds of her kimono closer about her. Even so, she was intensely conscious of the revealing thinness of her garments, and of the fact that her nipples were standing taut against the material.

'I should get dressed,' she said distractedly, half turning towards the door, but his hand about her wrist prevented her from leaving.

'Don't,' he said, his thumb moving insistently over the vulnerable inner veins, and although she knew he was probably unaware of what he was doing, her breath caught painfully in her throat.

The sound of footsteps crossing the hall outside made Shelley put some distance between them. By the time Marsha appeared in the doorway, she had taken a seat at the table, and the older woman looked at them delightedly, evidently sensing nothing amiss.

'Isn't this a surprise, Shelley?' she exclaimed, bustling into the room to set a third place at the table. 'I see you two have renewed your acquaintance. I'm surprised you recognised Dickon. It must be eight or nine years since you last met.'

'Eight,' said her son drily, returning to the chair he had occupied before Shelley's intervention. 'But Shelley hasn't changed. I'd have recognised her anywhere.'

Shelley managed a tight smile, but the look she cast in his direction was apprehensive. 'How gallant!' she said, her elbows on the table protecting her body from his gaze. 'Your son has inherited your flare for understatement, Marsha. It's very kind, but it's not the truth.'

Marsha laughed. 'Oh, Dickon has always been able to charm his way out of any situation,' she declared, not without a certain amount of motherly pride, and her son expelled an exasperated breath.

'My name's Benedict, Mother, not Dickon.' His eyes moved briefly to Shelley's averted head and then back again. 'I doubt if your guest even knows my proper surname.'

'Does it matter?' Marsha pulled a face at him. 'Shelley doesn't care if you call yourself Benedict Manning or Benedict Seton, and I, for one, prefer the name Dickon to Ben.' She shrugged. 'Benedict was your father's choice. I wanted to call you Richard.'

'Well, I prefer Ben,' he retorted, as the maid came into the room carrying a fresh pot of coffee and a rack of toast. 'What do you think, Sarah? Do I look more like a Ben than a Dickon?'

'Oh, Mr Benedict, I don't know,' the girl simpered girlishly, her eyes darting triumphantly in Shelley's direction, almost as if *she* might be envying her his attention. 'But Mrs Carr did say to ask you if you wanted sausages as well as bacon for breakfast. 'Cos if you do, I've got to run down to the village and see if Mrs Peart's is open.'

'Bacon is fine,' Ben assured her firmly, and his mother pursed her lips.

'Honestly, that girl is impossible sometimes,' she exclaimed, after Sarah had left the room. 'And you encourage her, Dickon. You know perfectly well she was not supposed to add that rider about having to run down to the village! If you wanted sausages, you should have asked for them. It wouldn't have taken her more than five minutes to ride down to the stores on her bicycle!'

'But I didn't want sausages, Mother,' Ben

responded patiently. 'I'm only having bacon because you insisted. Where is it, by the way? I don't have all day.'

'Oh—I'd better go and speak to Mrs Carr,' declared Marsha, pushing back her chair, and before Shelley could prevent her, she had left the room once again.

'You didn't tell my mother about me giving you a lift yesterday, did you?' Ben asked, as soon as Marsha was out of earshot, and Shelley made an involuntary gesture.

'How could I? I didn't know who you were,' she reminded him, deliberately keeping her tone light. But her stomach was churning and she suspected he was not deceived.

'Why not tell her just now?' he persisted, watching the delicate colour invade her throat. 'I assume she does know you snapped a fanbelt. She was very concerned about your whereabouts when I rang last night.'

'I told her what happened,' Shelley countered defensively. 'And that I'd been given a lift into Low Burton.' She tilted her head. 'Why didn't you tell her last night?'

'*Touché.*' Ben acknowledged her offensive with a wry smile. 'For the same reasons you didn't, I suppose,' he replied softly. 'I didn't want to talk about it. Not then, anyway.'

Shelley felt as if she was losing her grip on the conversation, and forcing a careless smile, she said: 'I suppose we both took the easy way out.' Dismissing the subject, she cupped her chin in her hands: 'Marsha tells me you're engaged to be married. How exciting! When am I going to meet your fiancée?'

'Don't patronise me, Shelley!'

The sudden anger in his voice was unmistakable,

and she pressed her hand to her throat in an effort to control the erratic racing of her heart. It was crazy to allow this situation to develop any further, and her mouth was dry as she reached for the pot of coffee.

'Do you want some?' she asked, hoping she would not spill it, but with a shake of his head, he got abruptly to his feet.

'I'll tell my mother I can't wait any longer,' he said, subjecting her to a devastating appraisal. He strode towards the door. 'Oh—and Shelley——' This, with his fingers on the handle and his temple pressed against the jamb: 'You're nothing like my mother, so don't act like her. And you haven't changed. You're still the most beautiful woman I've ever seen!'

CHAPTER THREE

THE following evening, Shelley examined her reflection with some misgivings. Was what she was wearing suitable for a simple family dinner, she wondered. The dark blue Dior silk was very plain, but it was also very flattering, and the last thing she wanted to do was look as if she was trying too hard. The dress was cut with style and elegance, moulding the seductive fullness of her breasts and flaring over her slim hips. It had seemed the most appropriate choice in her wardrobe, but now she was not so sure. Marsha had said any old thing would do, but Shelley didn't have 'any old thing'. Most of her clothes were expensive, bought with her position in mind. She could hardly appear in a shirt and jeans when she was going to meet Ben's fiancée.

Turning away from the mirror, Shelley cast an abstracted look about the bedroom. Where had she put her shoes? And thank goodness she had done her make-up earlier. Right now, she knew her hands were shaking, and any attempt to apply the dusky amber eyeshadow and burnt coral lip-gloss would have surely ended in disaster. Her hair, too, had benefited from the wax conditioning she had given it before her shower. Now, knotted securely on top of her head, it gave her height and confidence, even its colour muted by the severe style. She looked her age, she thought reassuringly, glancing at her reflection once again. She was completely unaware that by twisting back her hair, she had exposed the porcelain-like purity of her profile.

The sound of a car outside brought her swiftly to the window, but she concealed herself behind the curtain when a dark red Porsche drew round in a circle and came to a halt on the forecourt. Feeling horribly like one of those women who live their lives through observing others, Shelley would have turned away then, if Marsha's son had not immediately emerged from the vehicle. In beige corded pants and a matching jacket, he looked every bit as disturbing as she remembered, the breeze lifting the thick swathe of sun-bleached hair and depositing several strands across his forehead.

Oh, dear! she thought unsteadily, feeling the bones of her shoulders digging into the wall behind her. This was madness! But she could not tear her eyes away as he walked round the car and opened the door for the girl at the other side.

Jennifer Chater was wearing a strappy sundress, which exposed the warm-brown skin of her arms and throat. Her hair was dark, a curly halo around her head, and although she was not tall, she was nicely proportioned, with vivacious features, narrow hips, and small high breasts. But most of all, she looked *young*, and Shelley breathed a sigh of relief. Nothing could point the differences between them more than to compare the wrap-around décolletage and narrow sleeves of her sophisticated—no, *mature*—gown with Jennifer's candy-striped cotton. Shelley looked elegant, but Jennifer looked fresh and youthful, the veneer of girlish innocence not yet tarnished by experience. And she was evidently in love with Ben, unable to prevent herself from clinging to his arm as they circled the car and came into the house. Lucky girl, thought Shelley tautly, as she moved back into the room. But not before noticing that Ben lifted his eyes to her windows, as he passed beneath, and her ragged nerves reacted anew to the possibility that he might have seen her.

She had to go down. She knew it. But that didn't make it any easier. Marsha had said they would eat at seven-thirty, and that Ben and Jennifer would arrive a little earlier, so they could all have a drink beforehand. It was almost twenty-five past seven now. She couldn't delay any longer. They would think she had planned to make an entrance.

A final check that her tights were smooth, and that the hem of her dress was not too short for a woman of almost thirty-one, Shelley left her room and went down the stairs. Her perfume, a delicate fragrance by Yves Saint Laurent, encircled her in its aura, and she drew a little comfort from the fact that she looked, *and smelt*, like a successful female executive. It was ridiculous to allow a young man of Ben Seton's age to upset her, she thought impatiently. Obviously, her precarious mental state had produced other complications. Tonight, she would prove she was definitely on the mend.

She heard the sound of voices coming from the library, and steeling herself for that initial entry, she walked across the hall with her head held high. The door was open, making it easier for her to step inside unnoticed, she thought, but Marsha would not let it happen.

'Shelley!' she exclaimed, immediately drawing the attention of the other three occupants of the room, and now Shelley saw there was another man present. Tall and dark and distinguished, with flecks of grey marking the line of his temples, the newcomer was regarding her with evident approval, and Marsha was not unaware of this as she moved to greet her friend. 'Don't you look lovely!'

she exclaimed generously, dismissing Shelley's admiration of her own silk blouse and velvet skirt without enthusiasm. 'Come along. Jennifer and Charles are dying to meet you. I told you Charles was joining us, didn't I? Charles Brandeth, our local G.P.?'

'You know you didn't, Marsha,' responded Shelley, in a low voice, and Marsha's eyes danced.

'Oh, well—come and meet him now,' she invited incorrigibly. 'He's a widower, actually. His wife died several years ago. He has no family, and he's awfully nice.'

'Marsha!' murmured Shelley warningly, but she had no choice than to go and be introduced, first to Ben's fiancée, and then to the village doctor.

Conscious that Ben's eyes had been on her from the moment she came into the room, Shelley was careful to look only at Jennifer as they were introduced. She was a pretty little thing, Shelley conceded, aware that her opinion would not bear closer scrutiny, and she would probably make Ben an ideal wife. Being a veterinary's daughter, she already knew the odd hours he would have to work, and no doubt she was prepared for the demands his job would make on their lives.

'I believe you and Ben's mother are old friends,' she said now, after they had shaken hands, and Shelley immediately felt her age. 'How long are you staying? Don't you find Craygill rather boring after the exciting life you must have in London?'

'Oh, Jennifer, don't say that!' exclaimed Marsha, making light of the girl's rather tactless comments. 'I'm hoping Shelley will stay all summer. If you start reminding her of what she's missing in London, I shan't stand a chance!'

'I'm sure Miss Hoyt is appreciating the benefit of our rustic charms, Marsha,' Charles Brandeth intervened smoothly. 'How are you this evening, Miss Hoyt? I've been looking forward to making your acquaintance.'

'Thank you.'

Shelley managed a small smile, and as Jennifer turned away to speak to Marsha, Ben took her place. His hand beneath her elbow sent tremors of apprehension up her arm, and his voice was disruptively intimate as he said: 'Come and get a drink. I want to talk to you.'

'I—can't.' Shelley's breath caught in her throat as she looked at him. The message in his eyes was quite unmistakable, and although for the past two days she had been trying to convince herself that the compliment he had paid her when he was leaving the other morning had been objective, she could no longer delude herself that this was so. 'Ben—*please*——'

'Are you getting Shelley a drink, Dickon?' enquired his mother behind them, and Jennifer started to laugh at something Charles had said. With a feeling of relief, Shelley moved so that Ben was forced to release her, and the situation resumed perspective as she restored a sense of balance.

'You'll never believe it, darling,' exclaimed Jennifer, unaware that she did not have her fiancé's undivided attention, 'but Charles has just been telling me that Mrs Simmons called him out to look at Arthur! Arthur is Mrs Simmons' cat,' she added, for their guest's benefit. 'Isn't it priceless! She behaves as if that cat was human!'

'She's a lonely old woman,' responded Ben tersely, responding to his mother's frantic gestures, and crossing the room to where a tray of drinks was waiting. 'What will you have, Shelley? I think we've got most things here.'

'A—glass of white wine would be lovely,' replied Shelley nervously, linking her hands together. Then, finding his fiancée's eyes upon her, she added quickly: 'What do you do—er—Jennifer? Do you work with Ben and your father?'

'No.' Jennifer shook her head. 'I work in a solicitor's office actually. But I expect I'll give that up after we're married. Ben will need someone to answer his calls and take messages. Both Daddy and Uncle Bill are near to retirement, and when they do, Ben will be the senior partner in the practice.'

'I see.'

Shelley was nodding as Ben joined them with her drink, his fingers brushing hers as he handed her the glass. His hands were cool and hard, but they burned Shelley's flesh, and she wondered if he was as aware as she was of the electricity flowing between them.

'I was just telling Shelley that when Daddy and Uncle Bill retire, you'll be taking on a junior partner,' said Jennifer, taking hold of his arm, as if she couldn't bear not to be in contact with him. 'We're getting married in October. You must come to the wedding.'

'Oh—I—that's very nice of you, but——'

'It's not a definite date,' said Ben flatly, as Shelley struggled to find words to excuse herself. 'It really depends on Jennifer's father. You do want him to be at the wedding, don't you?' he added, as the girl clinging to his arm started to protest.

'Well, of course I do, but——'

'Dickon, don't be so aggressive!' Marsha came to soothe Jennifer's ruffled feelings. 'Honestly, these two!' she exclaimed, to no one in particular. 'They can't even agree on a date for their own wedding!'

'Personally, I have a great respect for elopements,' put in Charles Brandeth provokingly. 'No guests; no fuss; no——'

'——thanks!' declared Marsha, putting an end to his pronouncement. 'You wouldn't want to cheat me out of my part in my only son's nuptials, would you? I want to see Dickon in a morning suit, Charles, walking down the aisle of the church in Low Burton. And Jennifer, of course. My dear, you'll look delightful in white with your dark hair.'

'Mummy's already seen a dress she thinks would suit me,' put in Jennifer eagerly. 'It's in Harrogate. Maybe you'd like to come with us one day to see it, Mrs Seton. I know Mummy would appreciate your opinion.'

Shelley sipped her wine as the conversation ebbed and flowed around her. She took little part in it, and she was glad to withdraw inside herself and assimilate her position. Even so, she couldn't help but notice that Ben spoke seldom also, and she was half afraid someone else would notice the intentness of his eyes when they rested upon her. She was imagining things, she told herself. She *had* to be. But the fact remained that he disturbed her in a way she found quite intolerable.

Sarah's appearance, to announce that dinner was served, interrupted her troubled speculations, and Ben's mother was not slow to notice that the maid's eyes lingered longest on her son. 'Shall we go in?' she suggested, touching Shelley's sleeve and drawing her with her. 'Really, that girl!' she added, in an undertone. 'It doesn't seem to occur to her that *I* might object!'

'Object?' Shelley moistened her lips. 'What do you mean?'

'Sarah,' hissed Marsha impatiently. 'Haven't

you noticed the covetous glances she keeps directing at Dickon? I keep telling myself she's only seventeen and doesn't know any better, but she's beginning to annoy me.'

'Oh.' Shelley felt a chill run down her spine. 'I see.'

'I blame Dickon partly,' Marsha added, as they entered the dining room. 'I mean—he teases the girl and she takes him seriously. But he is engaged now, and Sarah should realise he's not interested in her!'

'Yes.'

Shelley absorbed what the other woman was saying with a distinctly hollow feeling. She wondered if Marsha would be confiding in her if she suspected Shelley's own involvement. Unwilling, perhaps, but none the less fundamental because of that.

Struggling with her conscience, Shelley tried to pay attention to her surroundings. The dining table looked lovely. Mrs Carr had arranged the place settings on Venetian lace mats, and the china and cutlery was reflected in the table's polished surface. Scarlet napkins tucked into crystal goblets marked every place, and a centrepiece of roses and carnations seemed to oscillate in the glow of two tall candles.

'It's really not dark enough to need the candles, but I thought they looked pretty,' remarked Marsha, directing everyone to their seats. 'Shelley—you sit here beside me, with Charles next to you, and Jennifer, you sit opposite Shelley.' She smiled up at her son. 'I'm sure you can find your own place, darling.'

With Marsha occupying the principal position at the head of the table, Shelley found herself almost opposite Ben as he took his place beside his fiancée. Marsha had arranged it so that as Charles had no one else beside him, he was obliged to talk to Shelley, and throughout the start of the meal, she seemed to spend her time answering his questions.

'It must be very interesting, working in the media,' he eventually commented predictably, and Shelley, who was used to this kind of query, gave a practised smile.

'I like it,' she said, though without the enthusiasm she had once possessed. 'Any kind of communication is important in a society that seems to spend its time withdrawing from human contact.'

'Is that what we do?' Charles arched his rather heavily marked brows. 'What makes you think so?'

'Oh——' Shelley was loath to get involved in dogma. 'Isn't it obvious? Every aim of Western civilisation seems designed to discommunicate man from his neighbour. The age of the computer signalled the start of increasing isolation.'

'Do go on.' Charles was intrigued, but Shelley was reluctant. A gap had occurred in the conversation Marsha had been having with Jennifer, and now everyone's attention was focused on her.

'I'm sure you don't want to hear my views,' she averred, in some embarrassment, endeavouring to swallow a piece of asparagus that seemed to have lodged in her throat. She took a mouthful of her wine, wishing she had made some non-committal comment, and then was immeasurably grateful when Ben intervened.

'I think what Shelley means is that computers are set to make a drastic change in our lifestyle,' he remarked. 'Right now, we are barely scraping the surface of what they can do for us. I was reading the other day, that by the turn of the century computers will handle a household budget, re-ordering any commodity as its needed from another computer at a store. They're even talking of computers that can diagnose simple illnesses, to save doctors making house calls. You'd better watch out, Charles. You could be out of a job.'

'Not me.' Charles grimaced. 'By that time, I'll have retired, thank God!' He shook his head. 'It's a frightening thought though, isn't it? No need to go shopping; no need to visit your doctor. I guess it all began when the cinemas started to close.'

'For which we can thank television,' said Ben drily, and Shelley, who had disposed of the asparagus at last and was beginning to relax again, caught her breath. 'You can't avoid the fact that television has a lot to answer for,' he added, holding her gaze with lazy irony. 'Wasn't it the medium that started this lack of communication? I seem to remember it being accused of killing the art of conversation.'

'Well, yes. But people are better informed because of it,' exclaimed Shelley defensively. 'Do you have any idea how many prospective voters are reached at election time, by the simple formula of networking a politician's views?'

'And do you think that's a good thing?' enquired Ben sardonically. 'Do you think it's fair to expose the ordinary man in the street to a stream of fanatics spouting their own particular brand of insanity?'

'People are free to choose,' protested Shelley. 'They can always turn the set off. They don't have to listen.'

'But they do.' Ben arched one eyebrow. 'Aren't you forgetting? Not everyone is mentally capable of deciding what to believe and what not?'

'That's a very supercilious statement——'

'It's realistic——'

'It's intellectual snobbery!'

'So you'd let anyone hear—or see—anything?'

Shelley flushed. 'I'm not saying that.'

'What are you saying then?'

'I've heard that some entertainers refuse to appear on the box because it kills their material,' put in Charles soothingly. 'What kind of programming are you involved in, Shelley? Does light entertainment come into your sphere?'

'Oh, really!' Jennifer raised her eyes heavenward. 'I'm sure Shelley didn't come here to spend her time defending what she does, Ben. She probably finds talking about her work just as boring as I do! This is a dinner party—not a political debate!'

There was a pregnant silence after this pronouncement, and Shelley wished the floor would open up and swallow her. She had not wanted to talk about her work; she never did. But it was difficult to avoid the inevitable interest it inspired.

'I'm sorry——' she was beginning awkwardly, when once again Ben came to her rescue.

'It was my fault,' he said, giving her a rueful smile. 'I'm afraid you're probably right. I am supercilious.' He glanced at Marsha. 'That's what comes of being my mother's son.'

'Don't involve me in this,' exclaimed Marsha, glad to use his words to ease the situation, and Sarah's appearance to clear the plates, provided a welcome diversion.

The conversation moved to the wine, and Marsha's preference for French vintages. 'Well, I may not be a purist like you,' said Charles, 'but I prefer the German wines myself. Did I tell you I've been invited to join a wine-tasting tour of the Rhine valley in October?'

'No, you didn't.'

Marsha was fascinated, and Shelley was relieved to be able to apply herself to the slice of lamb on her plate. She would have liked to take no further part in the conversation, but Jennifer decided otherwise.

Apparently sensing her fiancé's hostility towards her, she leant across the table and said confidingly: 'I hope I didn't offend you just now. But you did come up here to get away from your work, didn't you? Mrs Seton says you need a complete rest, that you haven't to do anything at all for at least three months!'

Shelley laid down her knife and fork. Put like that, it sounded as if she was on the verge of enforced retirement. She supposed Jennifer meant well, but she couldn't help the unwilling suspicion that the girl was using every opportunity to point out the differences between them—not least, the fact that she was young and energetic, while Shelley was old and wearing out fast.

'Not quite that,' Shelley said now, cradling her glass between her fingers. 'I just have to take things easy for a while. I've been—overworking.'

'She's not an invalid!' said Ben shortly, regarding his fiancée with impatient eyes. 'Mental stress involves the brain, not the body!'

'I know that.' Jennifer returned his gaze defensively. 'But you have to admit—Shelley—does look tired. And pale. She's not well. Anyone can see that.'

Ben looked down at his plate. 'She looks all right to me,' he replied flatly, and then turned his head to look at his mother. 'By the way, did I tell you I saw Martin Ashcombe on Tuesday? He says he'll be happy to come and look after the garden. It's exactly what he needs to keep him occupied.'

'Oh, good!'

As Marsha exclaimed her relief at finding a gardener, Shelley allowed the breath she had scarcely realised she was holding to escape her. But she was aware that Jennifer was still watching her with a faintly resentful air, and she wondered if the girl was preparing another offensive.

Refusing a dessert of fresh strawberries and cream, Shelley was relieved when she could leave the table and accept Charles's escort outdoors. Coffee and liqueurs were served in the garden, on a wrought iron table set on the sloping lawns, where the scent of honeysuckle and stocks filled the air with their sweetness. Cushioned garden chairs had been set nearby, and the sun's warmth still lingered on their framework.

Charles installed Shelley in a sheltered corner, and then went to get them both some coffee. As Marsha was busy with the cups and Jennifer was helping her, Shelley was aware that Ben was alone, too, and catching her unwary eye, he strolled across to where she was sitting. Squatting down beside her, he attracted her attention by the simple method of stroking his finger along her forearm, and she drew her arm away to avoid his disturbing touch.

'How do you feel—really?' he asked, his eyes dark and intent, and Shelley managed a slight laugh.

'You mean—because I look so—pale and tired?' she countered tautly. 'Oh—I'll survive. I'll just keep on taking the tablets!'

'That's not what I meant and you know it,' he retorted harshly. 'It's been rough for you; I know that. And if you do look pale and tired, it's not an unattractive disposition.'

Shelley bent her head. 'Oughtn't you to be

helping your fiancée with the coffee?' she suggested carefully. 'Charles is getting mine. I think your mother has asked him to look after me.'

'I'm sure she did.' Ben's tone was flat. 'What do you think of him?'

Shelley lifted her shoulders. 'He's—a charming man.'

'You realise my mother is trying to play matchmaker, don't you?' Ben declared shortly. 'She's hoping you may ultimately find Craygill more attractive than the big city.'

'That's not very likely, is it?' murmured Shelley steadily, fighting the insidious thought that in some circumstances it might be. 'I think you're exaggerating, Ben. Marsha knows my work is in London.'

Ben expelled his breath on a sigh. 'And you're a career woman, like my mother, right?'

'Right,' she conceded, looking nervously towards the group around the table. 'Oh—here's Charles with my coffee.'

In actual fact, Charles was still some yards away as Ben smothered a sound of impatience and got abruptly to his feet. 'We can't talk now,' he said, causing her to glance incredulously up at him. 'I'll call for you tomorrow. You can come with me when I visit some of the out-lying farms. It will give you a chance to see something of the area—— '

'No!'

'Why not?' His lean face was taut with exasperation, his eyes dark between their silvery fringe of lashes, but Shelley could not answer him.

'Here's Charles,' she said, as the sturdy doctor covered the remaining feet between them, and Ben permitted Brandeth only a brief acknowledgement before striding away towards the others.

'I suppose you've known Marsha's son for a number of years,' remarked Charles, subsiding into the chair beside her, and Shelley made an effort to drag her gaze away from Ben's retreating back.

'Oh—yes,' she responded, raising her cup to her lips with some uncertainty. 'He—er—he was still at school when I first met him. He's—grown up a lot since then.'

'Yes.' Charles nodded. 'He's a fine young man. And exactly the age my son would have been, had he lived.'

Shelley emptied her mind of other thoughts and gave him her full attention. 'Your son died?' She thought Marsha had said he had no family. 'When?'

'Oh—more than twenty-five years ago,' replied Charles reminiscently. 'Trevor—that was what we called him—Trevor died when he was a week old. I don't think my wife ever quite got over it.'

'I'm sorry.' Shelley touched his sleeve. 'What a terrible thing to happen!'

'Yes, it was.' Charles gave her a wry smile. 'Perhaps if we'd had other children it would have helped, but we didn't. Alicia—my late wife— refused to have another baby. It was such a shock to her, you see, after carrying the child for nine months.'

Shelley sighed. 'I don't think anyone ever quite gets over losing a child.'

'No.' Charles nodded. And then, with an obvious effort, he thrust his memories aside. 'But this won't do. I'm not supposed to be boring you with my troubles. Tell me, do you think you're going to enjoy your stay in Wensleydale? It may be quieter than London, but I can assure you, we have our own ways of enjoying life.'

Shelley was glad when the evening was over. Just after ten o'clock Charles reluctantly took his leave, in answer to a telephone message relayed by his housekeeper, and soon after that, Jennifer said that she and Ben should go, too.

'Ben's got to take me home first,' she murmured, linking her fingers with his. 'And Daddy doesn't like me to be out too late.'

'I'm sure he doesn't,' remarked Marsha warmly, exchanging a measured look with her son. 'Drive carefully, won't you, Dickon? These roads were not built for that car's turn of speed.'

'You can trust me,' responded Ben drily, submitting to his mother's kiss of farewell. His eyes moved to Shelley, and she forced herself to meet his disturbing gaze. 'Sleep well,' he said, and she wondered if she was imagining the intimacy of his words. 'I'll see you—both—soon.'

CHAPTER FOUR

SHELLEY was sunbathing when she heard the sound of a car at the front of the house. It was a glorious morning, and as Marsha had shown distinct signs of frustration over breakfast, Shelley had pointed out that there was no need for her to neglect her work while she was staying.

'Oh, bless you, darling!' Marsha exclaimed, giving up her half-hearted efforts at reading the newspapers and hugging the younger woman. 'I feel a heel abandoning you like this less than a week after your arrival, but I can't wait to settle down in my studio!'

'There you are then.' Shelley smiled, tossing back the chunky braid she had made of her unruly hair. 'I want you to stop regarding me as a visitor, and more as a rather grateful lodger. Honestly, I don't need to be constantly entertained. I'm enjoying just being lazy for once. I'm going to get a book and stretch out on a chair in the garden. You forget all about me!'

'As if I could do that!' Marsha touched her cheek. 'Oh, Shelley, I am fond of you. You don't know what it means to me, having you here. Stay as long as you like. I want you to think of Craygill as your real home.'

It wasn't easy for Shelley to relax after that. Although it was three days since the evening Ben had brought his fiancée to dinner, Shelley was dismayed to find she could still remember every word he had said, and whenever Marsha treated her with affection, she felt a hypocrite. She kept

51

telling herself she had no real reason to feel that way, that his words had been ambivalent to say the least, but it didn't work. She lived in a fitful state of apprehension lest he should appear again, and she despised herself utterly for allowing a— *boy*—of his age to disconcert her like this.

The vehicle's engine had stopped now, and levering herself up on her elbows, Shelley tentatively ran a tongue over her upper lip. It could be Charles, she told herself fiercely. He had called in the day before and shared their morning cup of coffee, but would he come two days running? Of course, it could be the butcher, who came out from Low Burton twice a week, or even the gardener, Martin Ashcombe, who Marsha had telephoned only the previous day. Or it could be Ben, she acknowledged heavily, swinging her feet off the padded footrest and curling her bare toes in the grass. And if it was, he should not see her like this!

She was halfway to the french doors that led into the house through the living room when he appeared. He came round the side of the building, eschewing the need to alert Mrs Carr to his arrival, treading silently in his mud-smeared rubber boots. He was wearing a dark blue collarless sweat shirt and tight-fitting jeans, both of which clung to the lean muscularity of his body, and his hair was moist around his temples, revealing an earlier bout of exertion.

'Hi,' he said, arresting her withdrawal, and Shelley knew she could not avoid his company.

'Hello,' she responded, turning reluctantly towards him. 'Did you want to see your mother? I'm afraid she's working at the moment, but I'm sure she'll want to know you're here——'

'She knows,' said Ben flatly, stepping off the path and on to the grass. He surveyed her appearance with narrow-eyed appraisal. 'As a matter of fact, she 'phoned me earlier. She was concerned about you, and she asked me to come and take you out.'

Shelley's lips parted. 'To—take me out?' she echoed.

'She felt guilty,' said Ben, stopping less than a yard away from her. 'She said you were being so understanding about her work, but that as you hadn't been out at all since you got here, you might appreciate a change of scene.'

Shelley looked anywhere but at him. 'But— that's ridiculous——'

'Why?'

'I told her. I don't need entertaining.'

'But I want to do it,' declared Ben quietly. 'So don't turn me down, hmm? Just go and put on a skirt or something, and let's go.'

'Like this?' Shelley was appalled. That morning she had felt so hot she had slipped on the sleeveless purple leotard she used to wear to aerobic classes in London, and without the tights that went with it, it was very skimpy. Already, her hands itched to tug the hem of the briefs into a more modest position, and it took an immense amount of willpower not to draw his attention to her discomfort.

'You look okay to me,' remarked Ben evenly, but she was aware of his eyes lingering on her breasts, partially flattened by the taut material of the suit.

'You mean, I look rather silly, and therefore less intimidating,' she said deliberately adopting her most patronising tone but Ben was not deceived.

'You've never intimidated me, Shelley,' he replied carelessly, and when she still refused to meet his gaze, he sauntered across to the lounger where she had been sitting, and stretched his length upon it.

'Your boots are dirty!' protested Shelley, forgetting all about her appearance as she went after him, and Ben looked up at her with mocking eyes.

'So don't keep me waiting,' he said, stretching out his hand and grasping her resisting fingers. His hand was cool and firm, the bones hard and determined as they curled about hers. 'Go on. Go and get ready. And don't take too long about it. I do have work to do.'

The appearance of Marsha settled the issue. She came out of the house just as Shelley was dragging her hand from Ben's grasp, and her delight at seeing her son made a nonsense of Shelley's objections.

'Of course you must go with him,' she exclaimed, when the younger woman expressed the contention that she was happy just to sunbathe. 'Really, Shelley, I'll be happier knowing you're with Dickon. And he doesn't mind, honestly. He'll be glad of the company.'

'Marsha, I told you——'

'I know, I know. You don't want me to worry about you. But I do. And if I know you're out enjoying yourself, I shan't feel so guilty about working.'

'Marsha.' Shelley sighed. 'Marsha, when you lived in London, I often spent hours at the studio while you were working——'

'But you weren't ill then——'

'I'm not ill now!' Shelley clenched her fists in frustration, as Ben, who had got to his feet when his mother appeared, gave her an amused stare. 'I just need to—to relax, that's all.'

'You can relax tomorrow,' declared Marsha firmly. She eyed Shelley's appearance critically. 'But I should wear something else, if I were you.

The farmers around here are rather conservative, with a small "c", and that outfit is definitely not!'

In her room, getting changed, Shelley flung the despised leotard on to the bed. She wondered what Marsha would have said if she had admitted that the real reason she didn't want to go out with her son was because she was afraid of what might happen. How would Marsha react to the news that her beloved 'Dickon' was not above making passes at his mother's friends? And more significantly, how would she feel if she learned that Shelley found *him* more attractive than was sensible?

When she eventually went downstairs again, Shelley looked as conservative as her clothes allowed. But at least the all-in-one jump suit covered her body and legs quite extensively, and only the elbow-length sleeves exposed a pale length of arm. The fact that the suit was made of a rather brilliant shade of jade green was regrettable, but the sheen of the material muted the colour as she moved. Her hair was still plaited in the braid. She had decided it was too much trouble to take it out, brush it, and secure it in a knot. Besides, it was hardly attractive as it was and she was aiming for a severity of style.

If Marsha had any objections to her appearance, she didn't voice them. Instead, she escorted them around to the front of the house where the Land-Rover was waiting, and patted Shelley's arm as she made to get inside. 'You'll enjoy yourself,' she said, but it was more a plea than a statement, and Shelley sighed.

'I'm sure I shall,' she replied gently, feeling obliged to offer the reassurance, and Marsha smiled gratefully as she stepped back to close the door.

*   *   *

Two hours later Shelley was wondering why she had been so apprehensive. Contrary to her fears, she was enjoying herself, and she knew a sense of shame for having doubted Ben's intentions. Since leaving Craygill, he had given her no reason to feel uncomfortable with him, and his behaviour and his manner had almost convinced her she had imagined his interest.

The scenery, too, had woven its own magic, and although the Land-Rover was hard and not absolutely sterile—though not as unpleasant as it had been that first afternoon he had given her a ride—Shelley bore its discomforts without protest. She could quite see why an artistic mind like Marsha's should find the tree-covered fells and rolling hills infinitely more appealing than the bleak grey streets of the city, and her own feelings expanded to encompass the beauty of her surroundings.

They visited several out-lying farms, which Ben said were cut off in winter, and where he had sometimes had to dig his way through mountains of snow to reach an ailing sheep. Now, after a spell of warm, dry weather, the farmers were complaining of the shortage of water, but they were glad to see Ben, and treated him with evident respect.

While he examined a bull that had damaged itself trying to reach a herd of cows, and diagnosed the reasons why a flock of sheep should have lost their appetites and become lethargic, Shelley was offered tea and scones, and plied with questions. It was obvious her appearance would arouse a not-unreasonable spate of interest, and she patiently explained that she was a close friend of Ben's mother's, and that she was spending a few weeks in the dale to recover from a period of ill health. It was easier to say she had had a debilitating attack of bronchitis than to explain the real reasons for her breakdown, and Ben eyed her a little wryly when one kindly farmer's wife offered her own remedy of vinegar, lemon and honey.

'I didn't know you had had bronchitis,' he remarked, as they clattered over the cattle grid on their way back to the main road, and Shelley grimaced.

'I haven't,' she said, pushing the bottle of linctus on to the shelf at the front of the Land-Rover. 'But I don't like talking about—well, about what really happened, and she was so kind I couldn't refuse.'

Ben nodded. 'They are friendly people. I've found that, too. Most dales people are. It's their way of life.'

'Well, not all,' said Shelley ruefully, and beneath his enquiring look, she found herself telling him about her early childhood, and of the farm at Tarnside, where her father was born. 'We never went back; not even for my grandmother's funeral,' she said, after explaining the hostility her father had encountered when his father died. 'I wrote and told them when my parents were killed, but they never replied. I guess they were afraid I might need their help, financial or otherwise.'

'Poor Shelley,' he murmured, his tone warm with sympathy, and she looked away. The sudden intimacy of his voice was like an abrasion of her senses, and she despised the automatic awareness that set her pulses racing.

'Are you hungry?' Ben asked abruptly, and she made a dismissive gesture.

'After being offered tea and scones at least half a dozen times, how could I be?' she answered lightly.

'But you didn't always accept,' Ben pointed out drily. 'I thought you might enjoy a glass of beer and a sandwich at one of the local pubs. Or, if you prefer it, I could buy a couple of pies and some cans, and we could have a picnic.'

Shelley glanced reluctantly at him. The idea of a picnic was very attractive, much more attractive than sitting in some stuffy bar, combating the fumes of cigarette smoke. And after all, Ben might not wish to take her into a pub where he might be recognised. No matter how innocent their expedition might be, she had the feeling Jennifer would not be enthusiastic.

'Which do you prefer?' she asked, making it his decision. 'I don't mind.'

'We'll have a picnic then,' said Ben, accelerating down the hill into the village of Garthwaite. Then, stepping on his brakes, he drew up outside the *Farmers Arms*. 'The landlady here makes a meat-and-potato pie that will make your mouth water,' he told her. 'Hang on a minute. I won't be long.'

When Ben came back, he was carrying four frosted cans of lager and two interesting packages. 'Two pies, and two slices of Mrs Marrick's famous apple cake,' he remarked, handing them over, 'And I know exactly the place where we can eat them.'

He drove out of Garthwaite on the road that ultimately led to the falls at Aysgarth. Some distance from the village, however, he turned the Land-Rover on to a narrower track that led down a wooded hillside. Twisting and turning, sometimes almost back on itself, it eventually emerged on a grassy slope, overlooking a rippling stream, where a wealth of forsythia and wild poppies grew vividly on the bank.

'What a beautiful place!' Shelley exclaimed,

unable to prevent her enthusiasm from showing, and Ben grinned.

'Pretty, isn't it?' he conceded modestly, and she pushed open her door and got out.

'Is this the start of the river we saw earlier?' she asked, walking to the edge of the stream, but Ben shook his head.

'Just a tributory,' he replied, joining her and lifting the four cans of lager out of her grasp. 'I'll put a couple of these in the water. It may look enchanting, but it's pretty cold, believe me!'

Shelley took a deep breath and then expelled the air from her lungs with real enjoyment. 'Do you know, I do feel hungry,' she said. She grimaced. 'I can't remember the last time I did.'

'That's good.' Ben dropped down on to the grass and held out his hand invitingly. 'Come on. Let's eat. Food always tastes better in the open air.'

Shelley didn't know whether his intention was to pull her down beside him or not, but instead, she handed him the two packages he had brought from the pub. Then, as he opened the bags, she seated herself on the bank, accepting the pie he offered without meeting his distracting gaze.

The pie was good and still warm, and she munched away happily, content just to enjoy the day. She didn't remember ever eating a meat-and-potato pie before, but it tasted delicious, and so did the beer. Ben had opened two cans and set one beside her, and from time to time she took a mouthful of the icy liquid. It was cool and sharp, a fitting accompaniment to the rich flaky pastry, and she licked her lips ruefully when it trickled down her chin.

The apple cake defeated her, but by this time Ben had finished his meal and his beer, and had stretched out on the grass. He had loosened the buttons of his shirt, which exposed his chest halfway to his waist, and he was presently scratching himself with a lazy hand.

'Did you enjoy it?' he enquired, turning his head towards her, and she wondered if he was as aware of his own sexuality as she was.

'Very much,' she answered, somewhat stiffly, struggling to combat the effect his lean brown body was having upon her, and with an indifferent shrug, Ben closed his eyes.

Swallowing the last of her beer, Shelley endeavoured to relax. It was very quiet, and very peaceful, and the measured sound of Ben's breathing had a soporific effect. Before long, Shelley could feel her own eyelids drooping as the rich food and the unaccustomed amount of alcohol made her feel sleepy, too. Perhaps she would just doze for a few minutes, she thought, putting the can aside and resting back on her elbows. It was very hot, and she hadn't been sleeping at all well lately. A nap in the sun seemed very attractive, and letting her elbows slide, she subsided on the grass . . .

She was dreaming—a delightful dream, in which she felt secure and loved. There was a man; she couldn't see him very clearly, but he was with her; he was kissing her; he was giving her this delicious feeling of warmth and security. It wasn't Mike. Mike had never made her feel like this. Even when he had made love to her, she had always known there was a part of herself that was not involved, that had stood apart and viewed what she was doing with a certain sense of detachment. But there was no detachment now—just an enveloping feeling of excitement and anticipation, that spread throughout her whole being in increasing waves of emotion.

It was the strength of these emotions that awakened her, and when she first opened her eyes, she couldn't understand where she was or what was happening. She was not alone; she realised that straight away; but the lips that were caressing the curve of her cheek were not familiar, even if the effect they were having was not unwelcome. A hand was pushed inside the collar of her jumpsuit, resting in the hollow between her shoulder and her nape, and the intimate caress of those fingers was what had aroused her latent passion.

'*Ben!*' As he lifted his head to seek the involuntarily parted softness of her lips, an awareness of her surroundings, and who she was with, swept over her. Turning her head away to obstruct his possession of her mouth, she exclaimed fiercely: 'Ben, what on earth do you think you're doing?'

'Isn't it obvious?' he enquired huskily. 'You're a beautiful woman, and I wanted to kiss you.'

'For God's sake!' Shelley could feel that she was trembling, but she pushed his hand away, and struggling up she added witheringly: 'Have you taken leave of your senses? You're not a little boy any more, Ben!'

'Does that mean you would have forgiven me if I was?' he countered flatly, levering himself up beside her. And then, more expressively: 'Eight years ago I wouldn't have dared. But that doesn't mean I didn't want to.'

'You don't know what you're saying!'

Shelley tugged distractedly at her hair as she stared at him, twisting the braid round and round in her fingers until her scalp protested at such careless treatment. But his eyes hypnotised her, their pale beauty darkened now by the frustration he was feeling, and it was difficult to be angry with him when what she really wanted to do was comfort him.

'Ben—I don't believe this——'

'Why not? Like you said, I'm not a little boy any more. I know what I want.'

Shelley bent her head. 'I think we ought to be moving on, don't you? I—how many calls do you have to make this afternoon?'

'None that can't wait,' he responded tautly. 'Shelley, look at me and tell me you don't want me to touch you.'

'I don't.' She lifted her head, but when she tried to meet his eyes, her nerves would not support her. 'Oh, Ben—don't do this.'

'Then stop me,' he said simply, cupping her face between his hands and lowering his mouth to hers.

She tried to resist him, pressing her lips together in a vain attempt to prevent his intimate invasion, but it was no use. The heat of his mouth and the probing moistness of his tongue overcame her inhibitions, and her lips parted helplessly beneath the searching pressure of his.

His mouth crushed hers as he bore her back against the grass, his hands shifting from her face to her neck, caressing the soft skin, bringing a trembling awareness throughout her body. The weight of his lean, muscled frame was upon her, the scent of his heated flesh was in her nostrils, and her arms moved up to his neck, and the damp silky hair that brushed her fingers.

His kisses became deeper, longer, more passionately demanding, and Shelley yielded completely to him. Her mind blocked out the reasons she was here, the trust that Marsha had in her, and the inevitable aftermath. For the first time in her life, she was responding wholly to her body's needs, and the moral outcome of her recklessness was something she was not yet prepared to face.

His hands slid down over her breasts and she quivered as his fingers sought the buttons of her suit, unfastening it to her waist and exposing the lace-trimmed bra she wore beneath. Then, with a groan he pushed the offending scrap of silk aside and buried his face against her creamy flesh. 'Shelley,' he muttered, his tongue seeking the swollen peaks she made no attempt to disguise, and his suckling lips started a raw physical ache, deep between her thighs.

It was at that moment Shelley knew she had to stop him, now, while she still could. She wanted him—*God*! how she wanted him, but it must not happen. If she let him make love to her now, she would be creating a situation infinitely more explosive than the one she had left behind her in London, and besides, she could not permit his evidently boyish crush on her to develop into something he would later regret. He didn't love her—heavens, he hardly knew her—he was simply working out a childish fantasy. But she was not a child; she was an adult; and she had no intention of allowing his undoubted skill at lovemaking to make her a victim of his potent sexuality.

Shutting her mind to the very real emotions he was arousing inside her, she forced herself to speak, using words she hoped might bring him to his senses. 'Ben,' she whispered. 'Ben, you're going to have to let me up. That beer you gave me—it's created a problem, if you know what I mean.'

There was a moment when she thought he wasn't going to pay any attention to her, when his lips left her breast to devour the bruised softness of her mouth, with an urgency bordering on anguish, and his movements made her aware of the hard muscle swelling against her stomach. And then, she was free. With a savage expletive, he dragged himself up and away from her, spreading his legs, and resting his elbows on his updrawn knees. With his head propped in his hands, his nails raking his scalp, he tore Shelley's heart, but she could not retract when so much was at stake.

'I'm—sorry,' she said, and quickly fastening the buttons of her suit, she sat up. Then, after making a tentative examination of her hair, she continued: 'I suppose we'd better go.'

'Had we?' Ben turned his head to look at her and his lips were twisted contemptuously. 'Don't pretend you meant what you said. I wasn't born yesterday.'

'Then you should know better than to question me, shouldn't you?' exclaimed Shelley defensively, realising she had to compound the lie. 'I'm sorry if you don't believe me, but that's the way it is.'

Ben expelled his breath scornfully. 'How convenient!'

'Oh, please. Don't let's have a scene!'

'Why not?' His silvery lashes veiled his eyes. 'Won't your nerves stand it?'

'Ben, don't be like this!'

'Like what?' He gazed at her without expression. 'Angry? Hurt? *Frustrated?*'

'I'm sorry about that——'

'I'll bet you are.'

'I am. But——' She cast about helplessly for something to say to ease the situation. 'Ben, it wouldn't be a good idea.'

'You've made that decision, have you?'

'Ben, it's not like you think!'

'You don't know how I think.'

'Oh, I think I do.' Shelley caught her lower lip between her teeth. 'You probably imagine I do this all the time. But I don't. I don't know what your mother's told you about me——'

'Not a lot!'

'—but I don't sleep around.'

'I'm not asking you to.'

'Yes, you are,' she retorted huskily. 'Don't pretend you only wanted to kiss me.'

'I don't pretend anything.'

'Meaning I do?'

'Well, you were lying weren't you? When you said it was so desperate that you should get away from me?'

Shelley was baulked. 'I—only in a manner of speaking.'

'What's that supposed to mean?'

'Oh, Ben, stop it.' She took a deep breath. 'I think we should go. Now. While we're still speaking to one another.'

'Why?'

She sighed. 'You know why!'

He shrugged, deliberately misunderstanding her, and rested back on his hands. 'So what's wrong with the great outdoors?' he taunted mockingly. 'If you are telling the truth, there's a clump of trees over there——'

Shelley drew a trembling breath. 'You're enjoying this, aren't you?' she accused, and his expression sobered.

'Oh, yes. Sure,' he conceded harshly. 'I always make a point of throwing insults at someone I want to make love with!'

Shelley pressed her lips together. 'Ben, I thought we were friends——'

'So did I.'

'And so does your mother,' put in Shelley fiercely. 'Can't you see what this would do to her, if she knew?'

'I don't answer to my mother any more, Shelley,' he retorted impatiently. 'For Christ's sake, what do you think I'm going to do? Go sit on her knee when we get back and tell her how *Auntie* Shelley has been teaching me how to——'

'Don't say any more!' With a cry of disgust, Shelley got abruptly to her feet and walked away from him. Her heart was pounding, and just for a moment she hated him for what he was doing to her. She walked blindly towards the stream, not noticing the huge briar until it tore painfully along her arm, and Ben misunderstanding, sprang to his feet, too.

'Shelley, come back!' he commanded wearily. 'If you really want—well, I'll take you back to the pub at Garthwaite——'

'No, you won't!' Shelley cast him a withering look, and then, without another word, she stalked past him back to the Land-Rover.

'What have you done?' Ben demanded, when he slid into the vehicle beside her and found her dabbing at her arm with a tissue, but Shelley was too choked up to answer him. 'Let me see,' he insisted, pushing her hands aside and examining the bloody scratch, and Shelley lost her temper.

'Don't touch me!' she snarled, her free hand connecting with his cheek, and he gazed at her incredulously before letting her break free.

'You are one mixed-up lady!' he told her roughly, raking back his hair with unsteady fingers, and Shelley shuddered helplessly, in the grip of emotions she had no wish to identify.

'Then—then you'd better not get *mixed up* with me, had you?' she responded tersely. And with the devil driving her, she added: 'What's the matter? Did Jennifer turn you down last night?'

A dull flush of colour invaded Ben's cheeks at

her words, and she knew a hopeless sense of remorse. She didn't want to hurt him like this. Dear God, she knew what she wanted to do with him, and it had nothing to do with the ugly, painful words she was uttering.

'Oh, Ben,' she began, almost on the brink of begging his forgiveness, when he interrupted her.

His voice cool and clinically detached, he asked bleakly: 'Would it make any difference if she had?'

'I—I——' Shelley was at a loss for words, but it didn't matter, for he answered himself.

'As a matter of interest, I turned her down,' he remarked flatly, reaching for the ignition. 'I haven't been able to touch her since that morning I came to breakfast at Craygill.'

CHAPTER FIVE

MARSHA came into the sitting room yawning and wiping her hands on a paint-smeared rag. 'I'm exhausted!' she announced, flinging herself into the armchair opposite Shelley. 'I really think I've worked myself out. I'm going to take the evening off, and to hell with it!'

Shelley smiled sympathetically, putting the magazine she had been reading aside and uncurling her legs from beneath her. 'Do you want some tea?' she asked, indicating the tray on the table beside her. 'Sarah only brought it a little while ago. It should still be hot.'

Marsha shook her head. 'She brought me some, too,' she averred gratefully. 'No. What I need is a hot bath and a nice relaxing evening. Do you know what's on the menu? When I'm working I lose track of everything.'

Shelley hesitated. 'You do know I'm going out this evening, don't you?' she murmured doubtfully. 'The operatic society, remember?'

Marsha grimaced. 'Well, I had forgotten, as a matter of fact, but that doesn't matter. I'm delighted you and Charles are getting together at last. You've been here two weeks already, and I was beginning to think you didn't like him.'

'Oh, Marsha.' Shelley crossed one jean-clad leg over the other. 'I didn't come here to accept invitations from men, no matter how attractive they might be.'

'But darling, you must admit, Charles *is* keen. He asked you to dinner last week, and then there was that weekend invitation to the pigeon shoot at Chilborough Hall——'

'Both of which I refused.'

'—and now, tickets for the Low Burton Operatic Society's production of *Camelot*!'

Shelley sighed. 'Just don't read anything into it, Marsha,' she begged urgently. 'I only agreed to go because I couldn't think of a reasonable excuse not to.'

'But why?' Marsha's face mirrored her frustration. 'You said yourself—he's an attractive man. And eligible. When his mother died, I believe he came into quite a lot of money. And that's apart from his salary as a G.P. He could afford to make your life very comfortable.'

'But I don't want to get married, Marsha,' exclaimed Shelley fiercely, getting up from her chair and walking tensely over to the window. Outside, a steady drizzle was falling and had been for the past couple of days. The weather had broken the day after Ben had taken her out with him, and since then there had been showers and blustery winds. That was really why she had finally accepted Charles' invitation; because it had offered a diversion. She had reached a point where she knew she had to do something before her feelings got the better of her, and going out with Charles had seemed the perfect solution. Until now!

'I'm not suggesting you should think of marrying him on the basis of your present relationship,' retorted Marsha now, watching her friend with some misgivings. 'Darling, all I'm saying is, you could do worse than consider Charles as a possible candidate. I should have thought, after your experiences with Mike, you'd be looking for a different type of man.'

'What type?' Shelley took a deep breath and turned to prop her hips against the windowsill.

'Oh—you know what I mean. Mike Berlitz was too—selfish; too conceited; too full of his own importance! Not to mention being married when you met him. It doesn't do to become attracted to men who are already attached.'

Shelley controlled her expression with difficulty. 'No?'

'No.' Marsha leant forward to help herself to a slice of Mrs Carr's fruit cake from the tray. 'Which reminds me, talking of attached men, we haven't seen Dickon for over a week.'

Shelley bent her head. 'He's 'phoned you, hasn't he?'

'Well, yes. But that's not the same as coming out to visit. I'm surprised he isn't haunting the place while you're here. He's very fond of you, Shelley. We used to talk about you a lot.'

'Did you?' Shelley didn't want to have this conversation, but it was difficult to avoid it. She forced a smile. 'I see you changed your mind about the refreshments.'

'Oh——' Marsha gave a rueful grimace. 'This is why I put on weight. I can't resist Mrs Carr's cooking. Even looking at her fruit pies puts inches on me!' She shook her head. 'I used to be like Dickon, you know,' she continued, turning back to her favourite topic. 'There wasn't an ounce of fat on me until I began to rusticate. I look at him now and I think, I used to be like that. It isn't fair!'

Shelley turned back to the window. 'What do you think I should wear tonight?' she asked, trying to reverse the trend once again, but Marsha was not to be diverted.

'Oh, you know you look good in anything,' she

exclaimed carelessly. And then: 'You know, you may see Dickon at the theatre. I know he and Jennifer had tickets, but I can't remember which night they were for.'

Shelley's throat dried. Marsha was determined to talk about Ben, and she could no longer avoid the fact that sooner or later she was bound to see him again. She knew why he was staying away from Craygill, of course, but if she intended to stay on here, she would eventually have to convince him he was wasting his time as far as she was concerned. That interlude by the stream had been a mistake, a situation induced by the drowsy aftermath of her nap and the alcohol they had both consumed. Ben had lost his head, that was all. He had been bemused by his physical arousal into doing things he would otherwise not have dared. And she had encouraged him—at least, initially—allowing him to touch her in a way which in retrospect seemed totally repugnant.

Even so, she knew she would never forget the journey back to Craygill afterwards. It had been the most uncomfortable journey Shelley had ever experienced, and she hardly remembered their arrival here, or her subsequent plea of a headache. She didn't know how long he had stayed, or what he had said to his mother over the afternoon tea Marsha had insisted on him sharing. All she knew was that Marsha had been very sympathetic to her after his departure, and there had been no hint that Ben had said anything to incriminate her.

'Are you all right?'

Shelley's prolonged silence had been noticed, and with a determined effort, she came back to the sofa where she had been sitting. 'I'm fine,' she asserted, regarding her friend with affection. 'Just tell me, why aren't you coming with us to the performance tonight? I'm sure Charles could have got another ticket, if you had asked him.'

'What? And spoil his evening!' Marsha chuckled. 'My dear, like I said, I shall enjoy an evening in front of the telly. It's ages since I watched a good play, and I'm sure I'll find something to capture my interest.'

The foyer of the small Druid's Theatre in Low Burton was crowded with people when Shelley and Charles arrived. 'It's quite the thing to be seen to be supporting the local arts group,' remarked Charles drily, as they edged their way towards the entrance to the stalls. 'Yes, good evening, Mrs Laurence! No, I haven't seen Dorothy, I'm afraid.'

Shelley had to smile. 'You're quite well-known, aren't you?' she murmured. 'Do you know everybody here?'

'I could say I recognise bodies not faces, but I won't,' said Charles humorously. 'And yes, I suppose I do know most people. I don't have many competitors in a community as small as this.'

'But you have some?' suggested Shelley, trying not to search the crowd too obviously for Ben's dark blond head.

'One or two,' conceded Charles, nodding and smiling at a group of younger women, who were eyeing his companion with undisguised interest. 'The local young wives club from St Catherine's,' he informed her, in an undertone. 'They're probably wondering who you are.'

Shelley grimaced. 'I hoped no one would notice me. I don't like feeling an oddity.'

'An oddity!' Charles gave a rueful laugh. 'My dear, you look quite beautiful, as always. And with your height and colouring, you could hardly go unnoticed.'

Shelley accepted his compliment gracefully, but she couldn't help the feeling that not all the eyes cast in her direction were so friendly. Perhaps she should resign herself to the fact that in a community like Low Burton she was bound to arouse curiosity, she thought. And even though the severely cut beige silk suit she was wearing did little to accentuate her femininity, its distinctive lines and understated elegance were obvious to anyone who understood fashion.

Relaxing a little now that it appeared Ben was not here, Shelley accompanied Charles into the auditorium, following him down the aisle to the front row of seats. A number of people were already seated, but once again to her relief there was no sign of Marsha's son. Charles saw her into her seat, and then excused himself to speak to an elderly man who had hailed him from across the aisle. 'Sir Malcolm Robbins,' he murmured, by way of an explanation, and Shelley studied the programme he had brought her while he went to speak to the local magistrate.

'Hello, Shelley!'

The unexpected greeting brought Shelley's head up with a start, and for a moment her heart thumped so loudly, she was sure it must be audible. 'Why—Jennifer!' she exclaimed, looking up into the girl's complacent face. Her eyes darted to the woman beside her. 'What a surprise!'

'We saw you come in,' said Jennifer, drawing an older woman forward, 'This is my mother. She wanted to meet you. She's heard so much about Mrs Seton's famous friend.'

'Hardly famous,' murmured Shelley awkwardly, shaking the woman's hand. 'How do you do, Mrs Chater. It's very nice to meet you.'

'Oh, it's my pleasure,' exclaimed Jennifer's

mother gushingly, although, like her daughter, Shelley suspected Mrs Carter did not welcome strangers into the community. She was about fifty-five, Shelley surmised, though she looked older, and there was a certain malicious edge to her smile, as if she regarded Shelley as someone she didn't quite approve of. 'Jenny says you're here to recuperate from an illness, is that right? I suppose it must be. I can't imagine anyone from London choosing Craygill for a holiday.'

'Oh, I wouldn't say that,' said Shelley smoothly, not prepared to let her have it all her own way. 'I love it here already, and everyone's been so kind to me.'

'We saw you were with Doctor Brandeth,' put in Jennifer slyly. 'I suppose Mrs Seton told you he's the most eligible bachelor around. Of your age, I mean.'

Shelley said nothing, and as if sensing her daughter had been too outspoken, Mrs Chater added, 'I didn't intend to be here tonight, of course. Jennifer was supposed to be coming with Ben, but there was an emergency call just before they were due to leave, and there was no one else could take it.'

Shelley expelled her breath cautiously. 'What a shame!'

'Yes, wasn't it?' Mrs Chater shrugged. 'Still, I'm sure I'll enjoy it. The operatic society has a very good reputation.'

Charles' return put an end to their conversation. It was obvious he had little time for Jennifer's mother, and after only the most perfunctory of exchanges, the two women returned to their seats.

'That woman sets my nerves on edge,' he commented frankly, when they were alone. 'I'm sure she's the reason her husband has had a heart condition for the past five years. I know that may sound harsh, but she really does make the poor man's life a misery!'

Shelley shook her head. 'That's the first time I've met her.'

'And the last, if you're lucky,' retorted Charles, with a grunt. 'Let's hope Jennifer doesn't follow in her mother's footsteps.'

Shelley managed a smile, but to her relief, the orchestra were filing into their places, and very soon the lights were lowered for the start of the performance. Yet, even when the curtain went up, and the stage was filled with the colourful costumes of the Arthurian era, Shelley found her thoughts straying. Had there really been an emergency call, or had Ben suspected he might see her here? she wondered, twisting the programme into a tight roll. And if he was avoiding her, how long could it go on before Marsha—and even Jennifer—began to suspect his motives?

It was about a quarter-past ten when the curtain came down, and the audience began to leave. An emergency exit had been opened by the orchestra stalls and, as they were on the front row of the auditorium, Shelley and Charles were among the first to emerge into the cool evening air. It was not dark. The clouds that had hung around all day had now dispersed to leave the sky clear and starlit, and only the pools in the gutters revealed it had been raining earlier.

'Not a bad performance,' remarked Charles, guiding Shelley round to the front of the theatre so that they could cross to the market square, where he had left his car.

'It was very good,' said Shelley, hoping she didn't sound patronising. 'And what a lovely evening! You'd hardly believe how miserable it was this—this——'

Her voice broke off abruptly at the sight of the man propped indolently against the bonnet of a dark red sports car. Parked by the entrance, he was evidently waiting for his fiancée and her mother to emerge, and Shelley's knees felt weak as she forced herself to walk with Charles towards him.

'Why—Ben!' said her companion, his greeting successfully covering Shelley's faltering words. 'We were talking to Jennifer and her mother before the show—or, at least, Shelley was. I hear you had an emergency call just as you were leaving. Hard luck! You missed a very pleasant evening.'

'I'm sure I did.' Ben straightened from his lounging position and thrust his hands into the pockets of his leather jerkin. He was all in black, and the sombre colour suited him, accentuating the lightness of his hair and the darker pigment of his skin. 'Hello, Shelley. Have you had a pleasant evening, too?'

'Very pleasant,' replied Shelley tensely, wondering if it was her imagination that was making his eyes look more deep set than usual. He looked tired, she thought anxiously, but that was probably because he'd had a long day. It couldn't be easy, being on call at all hours of the day and night. 'H-have you been working hard? We—that is, your mother and I—never seem to see you these days.'

Ben met her tentative gaze without expression, and she felt chilled. It was as if she was looking at a stranger, and while she kept telling herself that this was what she had wanted, she couldn't deny that his cold indifference was like a knife turning in her stomach.

'One of my colleagues has been on holiday,' he

said now, in answer to her question, and Charles, listening to their exchange, could have no idea of what was going through her mind. 'And as Jennifer's father is ill, I haven't had a lot of free time.'

'You should have got a locum in,' declared Charles at once, and Ben switched his attention to him.

'As a matter of fact, Joe Armitage's son qualifies in a couple of weeks,' he replied evenly. 'The younger son; Dennis. He's going to join the practice for a month or two, to see if he likes it.'

'Well, that will certainly take the pressure off you,' responded Charles, nodding. He smiled. 'We'd better be off. Shelley's shivering, and I don't want to be accused of creating my own patients.'

Ben offered a perfunctory smile, and Shelley, whose trembling had nothing to do with being cold, gave him a despairing look. 'You will try and come and see your mother soon, won't you?' she asked, wishing she could speak to him alone, and his lashes dipped.

'She understands,' he said, in a clipped voice, looking beyond her, and glancing over her shoulder, Shelley saw Jennifer and her mother approaching.

'Let's go,' said Charles, not wishing to get involved with Mrs Chater again, and Shelley had to accompany him.

'Goodnight, Ben,' she called, as they set off across the square, but she didn't think he heard her as he went to meet his fiancée.

Shelley parked her car in the municipal carpark, and bought the necessary ticket to display in the window. Then, after locking the vehicle, she walked back into the square, busy now with the bustling stalls of the open-air market.

It was Monday and exactly four days since she accompanied Charles to the Friday evening performance of *Camelot*. She had not seen him since, even though he had made an abortive attempt to invite her to dinner on Saturday evening, and she knew Marsha thought she was foolish for refusing his invitation.

'He'll begin to think you're playing hard to get,' her friend had asserted impatiently. 'There are other available females in Craygill and Low Burton——'

'Not least, yourself,' put in Shelley drily.

'—and I get the feeling Charles is beginning to regret his isolation,' finished Marsha imperturbably. 'It hasn't been easy for him since his mother passed away.'

'She died after his wife, I assume,' said Shelley, feeling obliged to say something, and Marsha nodded.

'Oh, yes. Alicia's been dead for more than ten years, but old Mrs Brandeth only died last July.'

Shelley had been suitably sympathetic, but Marsha either couldn't—or wouldn't—accept that she had no real interest in the widowed doctor. She was convinced Shelley's attitude had to do with her unhappy relationship with Mike Berlitz, and no matter how often Shelley denied it, Marsha still believed she was afraid of getting hurt again.

If only it was that simple, Shelley reflected, not for the first time, aware that getting hurt was not something one could always avoid. Given that alternative, she would not now be here in Low Burton, fretting over the fact that Ben had still made no attempt to see his mother, or contemplating the wisdom of approaching him on his own ground.

Wandering aimlessly among the market stalls, she tried to rehearse what she would say if she did see him. Phrases like: *Is it fair to punish your mother for something I did?* and *What do you think your mother would say if she knew why you were behaving like this?* sounded hollow indeed, when taken out of context, and although she couldn't remember that day by the stream without revulsion, she could hardly pretend she had been a wholly unwilling participant.

She had found Ben's address in the 'phone book the previous afternoon. When it became obvious that he was not going to accept the invitation to tea his mother had offered, Shelley had known she had to do something, and this morning she had fabricated a wish to visit the open market at Low Burton. She guessed Marsha would not want to accompany her. After a weekend of laziness, she sensed the other woman was eager to return to her studio, and Shelley was glad she had her own transport to make her friend's participation superfluous.

Marsha had felt obliged to offer to go with her, but Shelley had easily overcome her misgivings. 'I do know the way,' she declared firmly, smiling at the relief in the other woman's face. 'And I shall enjoy just poking about on my own. Is there anything I can get you?'

The only thing Marsha could think of was a bottle of linseed oil, which Shelley suspected had been manufactured for her benefit. But she had promised to do her best, and seeing a do-it-yourself store close by, she decided to dispose of that chore first.

'Do you happen to know where I might find

Ditchburn Lane.' she enquired of the shop assistant, as she paid for the bottle of oil, and the girl frowned.

'It's about five minutes walk from here,' she said, eyeing Shelley with evident curiosity. 'It's just round the corner from the Catholic church—that's St Winifred's, at the end of Farrgate.' She paused. 'Do you know where Farrgate is?'

'I'm afraid not.'

Shelley offered the girl an appealing smile and, as if taking pity on her, the young woman came out from behind her counter and went to the door of the shop.

'That's Farrgate, over there,' she said, pointing across the square. 'The one with Hobsons, the chemist's, on the corner. Just go down the hill a little way and you'll see the church. Ditchburn Lane is just beyond it.'

'Thank you.'

Shelley was grateful, but although she sensed the girl would have liked to know why she was making her enquiries, she managed to avoid an explanation. With a gesture of farewell, she walked away, feeling the girl's eyes on her as she hopefully melted into the crowd.

Farrgate sloped away towards the river, and St Winifred's church was some one hundred yards down on the right. Unlike the market square, there were few people about, and Shelley felt rather conspicuous as she passed the tree-sheltered wall of the churchyard. Her long-legged stride was quite distinctive, and although her open-necked shirt and matching tie-waisted white pants had looked quite conservative before she set off, she realised now that a darker colour would have been more appropriate. Even her hair, wound into a tight knot on top of her head, gave her an air of hauteur she had not anticipated, and she was half inclined to abandon her quest before Ben's neighbours became curious about who she was.

The lane where Ben's house was situated was a pretty, tree-lined avenue, edged by narrow town houses and cottages. Gardens, as full of colour as any she had seen, were reached through white-painted gates, and paved paths gave access to the dwellings. A striped tabby cat was sunning itself outside one of the cottages, and a dog rushed to the gate of another garden barking furiously. Shelley could have done without the unheralded attention, and she smiled a little ruefully at the old man who came to see what was going on.

Ben's house was the last house in the lane, the end of a row of terraced townhouses. It had a white gate, like the others, and geranium-filled window boxes, and an iron-trimmed front door in its narrow façade. The door was closed, and the place looked deserted, and Shelley's heart sank. She had hoped Ben might have returned home after taking surgery at the clinic, a schedule Marsha had been more than willing to explain when Shelley innocently asked about his movements. But it didn't look as if today he had kept to his usual arrangements. Surely either the Land-Rover or the Porsche would have been in sight, if he had been at home? And was there any point in knocking when it could only draw attention to herself?

'Are you looking for the vet?' enquired a curious voice behind her, and turning, Shelley found a girl of about seven looking up at her.

'I—well, yes,' she acknowledged reluctantly, arguing that a child of her age was unlikely to gossip. 'Is he at home?'

'Nope.' The little girl stuck her hands into the

pockets of her shorts. 'He's not come back yet. Do you want to wait in my house?'

'Oh—no.' Shelley shook her head quickly, accompanying her refusal with a smile, so that the child should not be offended. 'It—it wasn't important,' she assured her firmly. 'I'll speak to him some other time. Thank you for your help. It's saved me some time.'

'Do you have a pet that's sick?' persisted the little girl, and Shelley gave a rueful laugh. So much for avoiding complications, she reflected drily. It was obvious her inquisitor was as shrewd as anyone else.

'Er—not exactly,' she answered now, glancing apprehensively about her, but when she would have said goodbye, the little girl spoke again.

'Our budgie was sick last week,' she said. 'My Mummy thought he was going to die. But Mr Seton came to see him, and he said it wasn't a boy budgie at all. It was a girl. And do you know, she laid an egg!'

Shelley shook her head. 'Good heavens!'

'I know. Grandad said it must have been broody. Our chickens get broody sometimes. Would you like to see them?'

'I'm afraid not.' Shelley made a determined effort to extricate herself. 'Look—I've got to go. Thanks again. Goodbye.'

'Goodbye—oh!' The little girl's face creased into a smile of satisfaction. 'Here's Mr Seton now. Isn't that lucky?'

Shelley took a deep breath before turning to see the Land-Rover approaching fast. Her companion waved in delight, but Shelley was no longer so certain that she was doing the right thing. What if Ben refused to speak to her? What if her intervention merely widened the gulf between them? Her heart was beating erratically and her palms felt moist, and by the time the Land-Rover drew to a halt and Ben opened his door and got out, she was in such a state, she could hardly say a word.

'You've got a visitor, Mr Seton,' said the little girl, full of her own importance, and Ben gave her a fleeting smile.

'So I see, Linda,' he responded, raising his eyes to Shelley. 'This is a surprise. Is my mother with you?'

'No.' She moistened her lips and tightened her fingers around the bottle of linseed oil. 'I—came on my own.' She met his cool gaze squarely. 'Aren't you going to invite me in?'

Ben hesitated long enough for Shelley to know that without Linda's inquisitive eyes upon them, he might well have refused. 'Of course,' he said now, stepping past her to unlatch the gate. 'I don't have very long, but if you'd like to see the house, you're welcome to do so.'

Shelley bit back the defensive retort that sprang to her lips and preceded him up the path, glancing back at the child who watched them from the path. 'Your neighbour's child?' she enquired, just to be polite, and Ben nodded his acquiescence as he unlocked the heavy front door.

He stood back to allow her to precede him into the hall, and the heated male scent of his body was unmistakable. Although he was only wearing a cream cotton shirt and mud-coloured Levis, he had evidently been sweating, but Shelley did not find the faintly acrid smell of his skin unpleasant. On the contrary, she was immediately aware of how attractive he looked, and of how smooth and virile his flesh had felt beneath her fingers.

He closed the door behind them, and then led

the way along a narrow hall and into a room at the back of the house. Shelley saw it was a comfortably furnished living room, with a couple of tapestry-covered armchairs, and a matching sofa with wooden arms. The room overlooked the garden at the back of the house, only a part of which had been cultivated. Beyond a small lawn, the flower garden ran riot, and through the shrubbery, Shelley could see the unmistakable gleam of water.

'Is that the river?' she asked, moving towards the window, and Ben said it was. 'I didn't realise these houses were so near the water,' she added. 'You're very lucky. It looks really private.'

'It is,' said Ben flatly, still standing by the door, his hands tucked into the waistband of his pants at the back. 'Look, it's stuffy in here, and I've got to get a shower. Is there some reason why you've come, or was it only curiosity?'

'It wasn't curiosity!' exclaimed Shelley indignantly, putting the bottle of linseed oil down on a bookcase, and linking her hands together. 'Ben, please—will you stop looking at me as if I was some obnoxious specimen of humanity, and try and understand?' She sighed. 'I came because it's obvious you haven't forgiven me, and I can't allow your mother to suffer for something that was partly my fault.'

Ben's lips twisted. 'What do you want me to say?'

'Well—that you've forgiven me, of course.' Shelley spread her hands. 'Ben, what happened between us—it was a mistake! You must know that. I just wish it had never happened, and that we could still be friends.'

Ben lifted his shoulders in a careless gesture. 'All right.'

'All right—what?'

'All right. I forgive you.' He spoke offhandedly. 'Now, can I get my shower? I really don't have a lot of time.'

Shelley drew her lower lip between her teeth. 'Do you mean it?'

'Do I mean what?'

There was an edge to his voice now, and Shelley was not indifferent to it. 'Do you—do you really forgive me? I mean—you're not just saying it to get rid of me?'

Ben's nostrils flared. 'I really mean it.' But he didn't sound as if he did, and Shelley made a gesture of frustration.

'Will you come out to the house, then?' she asked. 'To see your mother?'

'When?'

'Today—tomorrow, this week!'

'If I have time.'

'If you have time?' Shelley caught her breath. 'Ben, you've got to make time. Or your mother will begin to wonder what has happened.'

'And that bothers you?'

'Of course, it bothers me.' Shelley gazed at him despairingly. 'Marsha's my friend. I don't want her to be hurt.'

'Okay.' Ben took a resigned breath, and gestured towards the door. 'I'll do what I can. But now——'

'I know, I know. You want me to go.' Shelley shook her head, and moved blindly towards him. 'I just had to come and speak to you, after the way you behaved the other night.'

Ben stiffened. 'I don't believe I said anything to upset you,' he declared bleakly, and she halted some distance from him to combat his accusing gaze.

'No,' she said, holding up her head. 'No, you're right. You were—excessively polite. I'm sorry. I shouldn't have mentioned it.'

'So why did you?' Ben raised one hand to support himself against the frame of the door, and in so doing successfully blocked her exit. 'What was I supposed to say that I didn't? You were with Brandeth. You evidently find his company more enjoyable than mine.'

'Oh, Ben!'

'Isn't it true?' His lean face was hard and unyielding, yet she could feel the tension emanating from him. 'My mother says he's invited you to dinner more than once, and didn't you accompany him to the pigeon shoot at Chilborough?'

'No!' Shelley denied the charge fiercely. 'Charles has invited me out, yes, but until we went to the theatre, I'd never spent an evening with him. I know your mother is hoping something permanent will come of it, but it won't. I like Charles, of course, but—but—sexually he doesn't—interest me.'

Ben's breath escaped audibly. 'Does anybody?' he demanded, his grey eyes darkening as they rested on hers, and Shelley felt her senses stir beneath his undisguisedly sensuous gaze.

'That's—not why I came,' she averred desperately. 'Ben, I just wanted to explain to you that, as far as I'm concerned, there's no reason why we can't go on as before. I mean——' She broke off as he removed his hand from the door and began to unbutton his shirt '—it's silly for us to—to treat one another like strangers, when we've known one another for so many years——'

Ben finished unbuttoning his shirt and pulled it free of his pants. Beneath the thin material, his skin was brown and filmed with moisture, and

Shelley despised herself anew for her totally uncontrollable response to his unconscious sexuality.

'Ben, what are you doing?' she mumbled helplessly, unable to look away, and with slow deliberation, he covered the space between them, and pulled her against him.

'Stop fighting it,' he muttered unsteadily, his hands sliding down her back to her hips, and as he pressed her against him, she felt the unmistakable proof of his arousal.

'Oh, Ben,' she whispered, half protestingly, but his mouth was on hers, and his tongue made a nonsense of her barely formed objections. Without hesitation, her lips opened fully to his, and her arms slid convulsively about his waist.

He kissed her many times, long, searching kisses that robbed her of any strength to resist. Indeed, she wondered if this wasn't really why she had come, after all. God knew, she had been desperate to see him, and in spite of all her good intentions, she could not deny the urgency with which she met his passion. It was heaven to be with him, heaven to have his arms around her, heaven to feel the pulsating heat of manhood thrusting tautly against his pants.

'I'm hot, and I'm sweating, and I need a shower,' Ben groaned at last. 'Will you wait for me?'

'Can't I come with you?' Shelley suggested huskily, and Ben looked down into her delicately flushed face.

'Do you want to?'

'Well, let's put it this way—I don't want you to leave me,' she admitted unsteadily, and with a groan of satisfaction, Ben swung her up into his arms.

His bathroom was small, and the shower cubicle was tiny, but Shelley didn't care. From the minute Ben had stripped off his clothes, she had been close against his hard body, and her own clothes were just an annoying encumbrance.

'Wait,' she whispered, as he stepped into the shower, searching for the cord at her waist, and with slightly unsteady fingers, Ben pushed her hands aside, and undressed her himself.

'Dear God!' he muttered, when she stepped into the cubicle with him and the creamy length of her body below the taut full breasts was revealed. Jerking her towards him, beneath the lukewarm spray, he let her feel the heat of his manhood probing her thighs, and she wound her arms around his neck, and brought his mouth to hers. His hands soon disposed of the pins that held her hair, and the tawny red curtain tumbled sensually about her shoulders. 'You are so beautiful!' he said emotively, his teeth skimming the soft flesh of her shoulder, and she raised her arm obediently, delighting in his touch.

But when she took the soap from him and began lathering his body, Ben could stand no more. Tossing the tablet aside, he turned off the spray and stepped out of the shower, and she wrapped her arms about his neck as he carried her into his bedroom.

'Won't we spoil the quilt?' she protested briefly, as the downy coverlet welcomed her damp body, and Ben gave an indifferent shrug.

'Probably,' he conceded, lowering his weight on to her. 'But right now, I don't care. Do you?'

Shelley didn't answer him. She couldn't. She was too busy responding to the feverish demand of his mouth, and her legs shifted sensuously, coiling about his. It was so satisfying to feel his warm flesh crushing hers, with nothing between them to mar the pure sensation of skin against skin. Her hands caressed his neck and shoulders, delighting in her ability to arouse his deepest emotions, and Ben moved sensuously over her, inciting a moan of anguish when his lips brushed the hollow of her navel.

His fingers slid between them, finding the moist entrance to her body, and Shelley's legs fell apart. 'Be patient,' he murmured, sliding back to find her lips with his mouth, and then the pulsing length of his manhood plunged deeply into her sheath.

'Oh, God!' she breathed, feeling him piercing her, filling her, possessing her so completely, she knew she had never experienced such an incredible sensation before.

'Is it good?' he asked unsteadily, as she arched her hips towards him, and her nails digging into his neck gave him all the answer he needed.

It was all over very quickly. They had both been aroused to such a pitch that Shelley senses spun mindlessly out into space only seconds before Ben spilled himself inside her. Even then, she was loath to let him go, and when he would have drawn away from her, she wrapped her legs around him, and linked her arms about his neck.

'You were—fantastic,' she said with a broken sigh, and Ben gave a rueful smile.

'So were you,' he assured her huskily, smoothing back the damp hair from her forehead. 'You're not sorry you came, are you? You're not going to regret this the minute I let you go?'

'No.' Shelley threaded her fingers through his hair, her expression delightfully content. She didn't want to think of Marsha right now, but she knew she could never regret something that had been so marvellously right. 'I just wish we had more time. I don't want to let you go.'

'We have plenty of time,' he told her roughly, turning on to his back and taking her with him, and amazingly she felt his length growing and swelling inside her. 'Come here,' he groaned, and she lowered her breasts to his hungry lips, as his hands curved possessively over her buttocks . . .

CHAPTER SIX

THE telephone disturbed them, pealing incessantly from the hall below.

Shelley, who had been asleep, wakened to find Ben dragging himself reluctantly off the bed to go and answer it, and she stretched out a hand in protest.

'I've got to get it,' he said ruefully, taking her hand in his and carrying it to his lips. 'I'm not on call, but it could be an emergency.'

'Hmm.' Shelley conceded his point. 'And if it's not?'

'I'll be back,' he promised hoarsely, drawing her hand to the moist strength of his body.

Shelley smiled, and with a muffled groan, Ben got to his feet. 'Don't move!' he ordered huskily, pulling on a blue towelling bath robe and, tying the cord about his waist, he left the room.

Rolling on to her stomach, Shelley luxuriated in the lingering warmth of where Ben's body had lain. The taste and feel and scent of him was all around her, and she lifted her arms above her head and dug her fingers into his pillow.

She had never felt so blissfully content before. She was at peace, replete, satiated by the hungry urgency of Ben's lovemaking, bathed in the glorious aftermath of physical perfection. It was as if she and Ben had been made for one another. They came together spontaneously, naturally, sharing and enjoying each other's bodies with a complete absence of inhibition. When Ben was making love to her, she could think of nothing else—*no one else*—and if she hadn't already realised it, she now knew what had been lacking in her relationship with Mike Berlitz. Mike had never possessed her soul. He had only touched her body. And even his lovemaking had been a paltry thing when compared to the ecstasy Ben could inspire, over and over again.

What time was it? she wondered now, as she heard Ben pick up the 'phone and give his number. How long had she been here? It had seemed such a short time, but the heat of the sun through the window seemed to indicate it was almost noon. *Noon!* With a gasp, Shelley grasped her watch and twisted it round on her wrist. Dear God! It was twenty minutes to one, she saw with horror. She had been here over two hours. Marsha would be getting frantic. She had said she'd be back by twelve.

Ignoring Ben's instructions, Shelley pushed herself up, and as she did so she overheard what he was saying. The house was small, and the 'phone was on the table at the foot of the stairs. It was impossible to avoid eavesdropping, and her tongue circled her upper lip as she heard his impatient pronouncement:

'I know I promised to take you to Richmond this morning, but—something came up. Yes. All right. I'll take you this afternoon instead. It's no big deal. I'll pick you up about two o'clock. Okay. I won't. G'bye.'

By the time Ben had replaced the receiver, Shelley had been to the bathroom and collected her clothes. He came to the bedroom door as she was fastening the buttons of her shirt, and Shelley didn't need to meet his eyes to know he understood.

'You heard,' he said flatly, heavily, his shoulder against the jamb, and Shelley nodded.

'It was Jennifer, wasn't it?' she asked, trying to keep her tone light. 'I seem to have interfered with her arrangements.' She pushed the hem of her shirt into her pants and offered him a rueful smile. 'I'm sorry. I didn't realise that was why you were in such a hurry. I home I haven't made things difficult for——'

'Will you shut up?' he demanded roughly, abandoning his stance by the door, and striding across the space that separated them. Overcoming the token resistance she offered, he hauled her urgently into his arms and buried his face in her hair. 'Mmm, you smell delicious,' he groaned, turning his face against her neck. 'And you taste delicious, too. I should know.'

Shelley couldn't prevent herself from responding for a moment, pressing herself against his muscled body and feeling his instantaneous reaction. Then, with a supreme effort, she drew back to look at him. 'I've got to go,' she said huskily. 'It's nearly one o'clock.'

'Is it?' Ben didn't sound particularly interested, and seeing the possessive gleam that entered his eyes as he looked at her, Shelley knew she had to take control.

'I must go,' she insisted, putting her hands against his chest, and pushing him gently, but firmly, away from her. 'Ben, you've got to get dressed.' She hesitated a moment, and then added: 'Jennifer could come round here.'

Ben's mouth twisted. 'That doesn't particularly bother me, right now——'

'But it will.' Shelley drew an uneven breath and stepped jerkily back from him. 'Look, your mother's going to send out a search party if I don't put in an appearance pretty soon. I promised I'd be back long before this.'

'Shelley——'

'Not now, Ben.'

With trembling hands, Shelley turned to the mirror that occupied the wall above a carved chest of drawers and hurriedly used the brush she found there. Her hair refused to respond to her hasty handling however, and after making several attempts to restore it to its knot, she finally made do with a roll at her nape.

She was aware of Ben watching her from his position at the end of the bed, arms folded, his feet slightly apart, the lapels of his bathrobe gaping to expose his lean brown body. He had never looked more attractive, and remembering how completely he had been hers only minutes before, she was tempted to give in to her baser instincts and keep him from making his date. But her conscience was already tormenting her for the way she had already behaved, and although she knew what had happened had been inevitable, that was no reason to compound her sins.

'You—you will come out to the house now, won't you?' she ventured, turning away from the mirror to confront him. 'I mean—your mother wants to see you.'

'All right.' Ben spoke indifferently. But, as she would have passed him to go to the door, his hand detained her. 'When will I see you again?' he asked, bending his head to brush his lips across her shoulder. His mouth burned, even through the cotton of her shirt, and her heart palpitated wildly at the unmistakable emotion in his voice.

'I—why—you'll see me when you come out to the house,' she got out chokily, almost prepared to abandon all reason and stay with him. 'God—Ben, I've got to go,' she breathed, tearing herself out of his grasp, and ignoring his impatient protest, she hurried down the stairs.

'Did you get the linseed oil?' Marsha asked, over a belated lunch, and Shelley's stomach plunged. The linseed oil! she remembered with dismay. It was still standing on the bookcase in Ben's living room.

'I—oh, Marsha, I'm sorry——' Shelley felt her face flame with colour at her guilty thoughts, and her friend gave her an apologetic look.

'My dear, don't get upset,' she exclaimed patting Shelley's hand. 'It wasn't that important. Good heavens, I can probably get a bottle of the stuff at Mrs Peart's, if it's necessary. I just wondered if you'd remembered, that's all.'

Shelley managed a smile as she forked a mouthful of honey-roasted ham. 'I didn't buy anything,' she lied, feeling a traitor. 'But I'll get you some this afternoon, if it really is a problem.'

'No, it doesn't matter. Like I said, it's not that urgent,' declared Marsha, watching her friend spread a roll with butter, and bite into it with evident enthusiasm. 'All I can say is, I'm glad to see your appetite has improved. It must have been all that fresh air. Where did you say you got to?'

'Oh——' Shelley blushed anew. 'It was a place called Arnbank.' She had actually passed the sign on the way home. 'I just toured around for a bit. And forgot the time.'

'Yes.' Marsha gave her a mock-disapproving look. 'I was beginning to get worried about you. I was actually considering 'phoning Dickon, and asking him if he'd go out and look for you. But he probably wouldn't have been at home. Bill Yates was due back from holiday today, and if I know Jennifer, she'll have been taking advantage of it.'

'Yes.' Shelley put her knife and fork aside, suddenly losing her interest in the food. Then, determinedly changing the subject, she added: 'What have you been doing? Working all morning?'

'Mostly,' agreed Marsha, as Sarah came to collect their plates. 'As a matter of fact, Charles called after morning surgery.' She grimaced. 'I know he expected to see you.'

'Then perhaps it's as well I wasn't here,' said Shelley fervently, running unsteady fingers over her hair. 'Marsha, I wish you wouldn't encourage him.'

'We've had this conversation before, Shelley. Heavens, you like him, don't you?'

'I suppose he's—very nice——'

'Talk about damned with faint praise!'

'—but that's not the point, is it?'

'What is then?'

'I keep telling you—I don't want to—get involved. With anyone.'

It was true, she told herself fiercely, silencing the mocking voice of her conscience. Just because she had given in to a totally natural physical need was no reason to go on punishing herself. She had not harmed Ben. He had wanted her, just as much as she had wanted him. The ethics of the situation were not involved here. She was a sophisticated adult, and so was he. They had used their bodies to give one another pleasure. In God's name, what was wrong with that?

'Shelley!'

She realised abruptly that Marsha had been talking to her, and gathering herself, she gave an apologetic smile. 'I'm sorry.'

'I was simply saying I'd feel happier if you could find someone to care about,' said Marsha gently.

'In some ways, you're such an innocent, Shelley. You worry me. I mean, here you are at thirty-one—or almost—and Mike Berlitz is the only man you've had any experience with.'

'I have had other boyfriends, Marsha,' murmured Shelley uncomfortably, but the older woman was not convinced.

'They were not serious,' she asserted, pausing for a moment to allow the maid to set the cheeseboard on the table. 'Yes, coffee for two, Sarah,' she conceded, without looking up, and the girl took her leave with evident disappointment.

'I have to be so careful what I say when Sarah's about,' Marsha added with a grimace, offering Shelley the biscuits. 'The girl is an inveterate eavesdropper. And I'm sure she'd like something to gossip about where you're concerned.'

'I'm sure she would.' Shelley refused the biscuits, but helped herself to a piece of creamy Cheshire. 'So do you mind if we change the subject? I'm not an innocent, Marsha, so you've no need to worry.'

It was a further forty-eight hours before Ben came to see his mother. The day after Shelley's visit to Low Burton, he 'phoned to say that Mr Chater had been rushed into hospital that morning with a suspected thrombosis, and Marsha didn't press him when he made no reference to his absence.

'Poor Jennifer,' was all she said when she came to find Shelley, who was helping Mr Ashcombe to pick some strawberries. 'It can't be easy for her, planning her wedding and knowing it could all be cancelled at a moment's notice. If her father dies, I can't see them getting married before Christmas, can you?'

'I don't suppose her father is too happy about it

either,' commented Shelley quietly, determinedly avoiding thoughts of Ben going to bed with Jennifer, and Marsha sighed.

'You're right, of course,' she said. 'I'm being selfish. I just don't want anything to go wrong, that's all.'

'Go wrong?' Shelley took the filled bowl of strawberries from the old gardener with a smile, and forced a note of enquiry into her voice. 'What could go wrong?'

'Oh, I don't know.' Marsha shook her head as they walked back to the house. 'I just want them both to be happy, the way two people can be. Not like it was with Tom and me. Or like you and Mike Berlitz.'

Shelley caught her breath. 'That's hardly the same thing, Marsha.'

'Perhaps not.' Her friend conceded the point as she led the way into the house. 'Well, let's hope Jennifer's father recovers. I haven't given up the idea of being a grandmother by this time next year, you know.'

Although Shelley spent hours preparing herself for Ben's eventual arrival, she could not have anticipated the impact his appearance would have on her. He arrived on Wednesday evening, just as she was coming downstairs for dinner, and she was intensely grateful Marsha was not around to witness her shocked immobility.

He came into the hall just as she reached the bottom stair, and her reaction to his physical presence hit her like a blow. He wasn't formally dressed. On the contrary, his thin knit shirt and sleeveless leather jerkin, worn over hip-tight denims, would not please his mother, but they pleased Shelley. He looked lean and hard and handsome—not in any gentle way, but taut and tough and masculine; and Shelley felt her senses stir in remembrance of how she had last seen him.

She halted abruptly, rooted to the spot, waiting for Jennifer's appearance behind him to bring her frozen limbs to life. She felt like a puppet, waiting to be jerked into action, and when Jennifer didn't appear, she felt her features harden.

Ben allowed the outer door to slam behind him, and then walked across the polished floor to where Shelley was standing. 'Hello,' he said softly, his eyes dropping intimately from her mouth to the dusky hollow between her breasts. 'As you see, I came. Are you glad?'

Shelley was immediately aware that the draped neckline of her cream silk shirt was too low, and that her brown velvet pants clung too sinuously to her hips. She had not dressed with Ben in mind; indeed, had she suspected she might be seeing him tonight, she would have worn something infinitely less flattering. But when he had 'phoned that morning, to give his mother a report on Mr Chater's condition he had said nothing about coming out to Craygill, and Shelley had relaxed.

Now, however, she was made insistently aware that far from assuaging the needs he aroused inside her, their lovemaking had only heightened her awareness of them. And, in spite of all her good intentions, desire was flooding her body in a wave of irresistible heat.

'Wh-where's Jennifer?' she asked, once more using his fiancée's name as a lifeline, and Ben's eyes darkened with sudden anger.

'What do you care?' he enquired brutally, and Shelley gasped.

'Of-course, I care,' she argued painfully. 'I—I wondered if her father had taken a turn for the worse, or something. When you 'phoned your mother this morning, you mentioned some new tests they were making.'

Ben regarded her broodingly for a moment, and then he thrust his hands into the pockets of his pants. 'He's all right,' he replied, lifting his shoulders in a dismissive gesture. 'His condition is stable. I expect Jennifer is with her mother. They need one another at a time like this.'

'Of course.' Shelley's tongue emerged to wet her dry lips. 'Please—give Mr Chater my best wishes next time you see him. And Mrs Chater, too. It must be a terrible time for all of them.'

'Yes.' Ben continued his appraisal of his booted feet for a few seconds more, and then he lifted his head to look at her with weary resignation. 'In any case, I wouldn't have brought Jennifer with me tonight.' His mouth hardened at her wary expression, but he went on harshly: 'For Christ's sake, Shelley, I didn't come here to talk about Frank's illness! All right, I feel sorry for him—for all of them—of course, I do. But I came to see you, and you know it!'

'No——'

'Don't be stupid! You know I did.'

'Ben, you mustn't say these things!' Shelley glanced apprehensively about her, remembering what Marsha had said about Sarah eavesdropping. 'Look, your mother's getting changed. Let me go and fetch her. She'll be so relieved when I tell her that you're here.'

'She'll have heard the car.' Ben's hand on her forearm prevented her from backing off, the hard strength of his fingers unbearably familiar on her flesh. 'Come into the library,' he said. 'We can wait for her there. I need a drink, and I suspect you do, too.'

She went with him because he had hold of her arm and because it was probably safer to argue with him there than conspicuously in the hall. Nevertheless, as soon as the library door had closed behind them, she freed herself, and put the width of the room between them.

'White wine, is that right?' Ben remarked, approaching the tray of drinks, and Shelley nodded. 'Thank you.'

'My pleasure.' Ben was sardonic, but when he handed the glass to her she made sure that this time their fingers did not touch. 'So?' he regarded her intently over the rim of his glass of scotch. 'What do we talk about? The weather?'

Shelley shook her head. 'Why not?'

'Because that's not what's on both our minds,' retorted Ben tersely. 'Shelley, we have to talk— and I mean properly.'

'There's nothing to talk about.' With a nervous shrug, she turned to look out of the window, concentrating all her attention on the delicate petals of a rose, growing in the border outside. 'Do you realise, I've been here three weeks already? I can hardly believe it.'

'I can.' Ben swallowed half his scotch at a gulp and took an impatient breath. 'They've been the most frustrating three weeks of my life. Except for Monday, that is.'

'Ben!'

'Well, it's true.' With an exasperated sound, he closed the space between them, his warm breath fanning the exposed nape of her neck. 'I've thought of nothing else for the past two days. Don't tell me you've forgotten how good it was between us!'

'No, of course I haven't forgotten,' she retorted in a low tone. 'And—and I'm not saying I'm sorry that it happened. But—it didn't mean anything, Ben. It was sex, pure and simple. I—I'd have thought that someone of your age would have appreciated the difference.'

Ben sucked in his breath. 'What do you mean? Someone of *my* age?'

'Well——' Shelley was forced to turn and face him, and supporting herself with her hands against the ledge of the window behind her, she said bravely: 'You do consider yourselves the liberated generation, don't you?'

Ben's mouth compressed. 'What has my generation got to do with it? You're the same generation as me, or had you forgotten?'

Shelley held up her head. 'It doesn't feel like it. Not when you talk like that. Ben, I'm six years older than you are——'

'Not quite!'

'Five and a half, then. It doesn't really matter. I—*feel* more like your mother's generation than yours——'

'Bullshit!'

'It's true!' Her nails dug painfully into her palms. 'And—and when you talk—about what happened, I think you should remember, I'm not the untarnished innocent you seem to think me!'

'What are you saying?' His eyes bored into hers. 'That I'm not the first man you've been to bed with?' His lips tightened. 'I know that. I know there was a man in London. My mother was worried about you and she confided in me.' He shrugged. 'I can live with that.'

'You don't understand——' Shelley was finding it increasingly difficult to sustain his penetrating gaze. 'Ben, please don't make the situation any more impossible than it already is. I'm your mother's friend! You're my best friend's *son*! We can't have a relationship. It wouldn't be right.'

Ben put his glass aside and moved in on her, imprisoning her between the cool wall of the window and the heat of his taut body. 'It feels pretty good to me,' he said huskily, bending his head to allow his tongue free access to the palpitating pulse at her jawline. And then, when she flinched away from him, he added angrily: 'When are you going to stop pretending that it's any different for you?'

'Because it is.' Shelley jerked her head away from him, her eyes bright and desperate. She ached to feel his arms around her; she ached to press herself against him and give in to the hungry demands his nearness was making upon her, but she couldn't. She owed it to Marsha to remember who she was—who *he* was—and allowing this situation to continue was inviting disaster. 'Ben, I think you should know—my—my affair with Mike Berlitz is not over!'

He stepped back a pace to look at her then, his eyes narrowed and disbelieving. 'No?'

'No.' Shelley crossed her fingers tightly. 'I—just needed a breathing space, that's all. And—and this holiday provided it.'

Ben's eyes darkened. 'I don't believe you.'

Shelley held herself stiffly. 'That's your prerogative.'

He frowned. 'Are you telling me you're going to marry him?'

Shelley shrugged. 'I don't know. Maybe.'

Ben's face was paler than before as he said: 'Are you telling me—it was as good with him as it was with us?'

Shelley hesitated, torn by the knowledge that he had inadvertently given her the means of his own destruction. She had only to say yes, and their tenuous relationship would be over. But did she truly want to do it?

They were still locked in that silent battle of wills when the library door opened, and Ben turned abruptly away. For a moment the bulk of his lean body was between Shelley and his mother, and Shelley struggled feverishly to regain her composure as the older woman came into the room.

'So there you are,' Marsha exclaimed, catching sight of Shelley's vivid hair behind her son. 'Dickon, what a surprise to see you. You didn't say anything this morning about coming to dinner tonight.'

'I'm afraid I can't stay for dinner, Ma,' Ben responded, after a moment, the brittleness of his tone evident only to Shelley. He kissed the cheek his mother proffered, and lifted his shoulders. 'Pressure of work, and all that.'

'Oh, Dickon!' Marsha was evidently disappointed, and Shelley wondered if he had intended to stay to dinner when he arrived. 'It's almost two weeks since you spent an evening with us. Surely Bill Yates can handle your calls for once. I can't believe you've driven out here just to say hello and goodbye!'

'Wheeler's mare is foaling,' said Ben, pushing his hands into the pockets of his pants. 'I promised I'd be there. And as his place is near here——'

'—you thought you'd call in,' finished Marsha, with a sigh. 'Honestly, Ben, I sometimes think your blessed animals take precedence over your own mother. I'd have thought that as Shelley was here, you could have made other arrangements.'

'Please—don't mind me,' murmured Shelley, with an involuntary gesture. 'I'm sure if—if Ben has made a promise——'

'There you are!' Ben spread a mocking hand. 'Your guest understands the situation better than you do. As a matter of fact,' he held Shelley's anxious gaze for an agonising moment, 'I'd go so far as to say, she'll probably be glad to see the back of me!'

'*Dickon!*' As Shelley's tortured breathing stifled in her throat, Marsha gave her son a puzzled look. 'What on earth has got into you? You know Shelley is always glad to see you—just as I am. For heaven's sake, I thought you were fond of her! But I have to say it hasn't been much in evidence in recent weeks!'

'Oh, Marsha, don't be silly!' Shelley was beginning to suspect Ben intended to expose her there and then. 'Ben has his own life to lead—and—and his fiancée's welfare to care about. You can't expect him to spend time with—with two old ladies like us!'

'You speak for yourself!' exclaimed Marsha indignantly, but Shelley's words had provided the necessary panacea, for Ben's mother at any rate. 'Oh, well, I suppose I can't make too many demands upon you at present. But I don't see why you should make Shelley the whipping boy for your impatience.'

'Can't you?' Ben's mouth twisted sardonically, but just when Shelley thought her world was about to come tumbling about her ears, he seemed to relent. 'Of course not,' he added, offering her a polite inclination of his head. 'I guess my attitude was uncalled for. Naturally I didn't intend to offend you. Put it down to—tiredness and overwork.'

Shelley nodded, avoiding his eyes, and without another word, Ben strode towards the door. 'When will we see you again?' protested Marsha, as he made to take his leave, and her son leaned wearily against the jamb.

'Soon,' he said flatly, flexing his shoulder muscles, and with another inclination of his head, he was gone.

CHAPTER SEVEN

As if the thought was father to the deed, Mike Berlitz rang the following morning.

Shelley was still in bed, laying claim to a headache that was almost as bad as she had alleged to Marsha, when Sarah came to tell her she had a call. The maid's lips curled a little at the other girl's hollow-eyed vulnerability, and her voice was offhand when Shelley asked who it was.

'It's a man,' she declared, briefly inspiring the treacherous thought that it might be Ben. But that idea was quickly dismissed. Sarah would have recognised his voice, and besides, after the previous evening's events, Ben was unlikely to try and get in touch with her.

'It's not Charles, is it?' Shelley mumbled, dragging herself up on her pillows. The last thing she needed right now was medical advice, however well meant, but Sarah shook her head.

'No, it's not the doctor,' she retorted, hovering by the door. 'I think he said his name was Berliss.' She grimaced. 'Do you want me to tell him you're not well enough to come to the 'phone?'

'Berlitz,' echoed Shelley, automatically amending the word, her spirits plummeting. 'Oh, God!'

'What do you want me to do?' Sarah was growing impatient, and Shelley made a helpless gesture.

'I'll come, I'll come,' she said, sliding her feet out from under the covers and groping for her kimono. 'Just give me a minute, will you? I'm not exactly with it yet.'

'No, you don't look so good,' commented Sarah, without sympathy, and Shelley met the girl's scornful gaze with a controlled stare.

'Thanks,' she said. 'I needed that,' and Sarah had the grace to colour as she went out of the door.

'You can take the call in Miss Manning's room,' she muttered, gesturing towards her employer's bedroom. 'That's the only room with an upstairs extension.'

'Okay.'

Shelley's head was throbbing by the time she picked up the receiver. Her own anxieties, combined with Sarah's scarcely-veiled hostility, were not a calming influence, and she was in no mood to talk to the man whose behaviour had indirectly caused her present problems.

'What do you want, Mike?' she asked, omitting the usual preliminaries, and her abrupt tone seemed to catch him unaware.

'Hey,' he protested. 'Is that any way to greet the man you love? I thought you'd be pleased to know I'm thinking about you.'

'Please,' she said. 'Don't let's start all that again, Mike. You know how I feel. I told you. And if that's why you've rung——'

'I rang to ask how you were feeling,' broke in Mike swiftly, before she could go on. 'Hell, Shelley, I've been worried about you. And when I got back from the States and found you were gone——'

Shelley sighed. 'How did you get this number, Mike? I didn't leave it with anybody but Dr Lanyard, and he——'

'I'm a newsman, Shelley. It didn't take much deduction on my part to guess where you'd gone. You and that termagent, Manning! You always were as thick as thieves.'

'Even so——'

'Her number's ex-directory? I know. But we have our methods, Shelley, as you should appreciate.'

Shelley's shoulders sagged. It was a relief to know that Dr Lanyard had respected her desire for privacy, but she should have guessed that Mike would seek her out, no matter what.

'At which point I should add that your shrink seems singularly incapable of grasping that I was—*I am*—concerned about you,' Mike continued. 'Okay. So things got a little tough. It happens to all of us, Shelley. Just so long as you remember I *do* care about you. And, when you've got yourself together again, you'll realise I'm right——'

'No, Mike!'

'What do you mean? *No, Mike*? Shelley, I love you. I need you. And now that Lesley's gone——'

'No, Mike.' Shelley could feel the familiar frissons of panic rising at the back of her throat. 'Please, I told you—I tried to make you understand——'

'To understand?' he echoed harshly. 'To understand what? That you led me to believe you cared about me, when my wife was alive and well? But that as soon as she became ill, and there was a remote chance that we might legally be together——'

'Mike, it wasn't like that, and you know it!' Shelley caught her breath. 'You told me you were free. You told me you and your—your wife—were separated; that you were waiting for your divorce to become final. I—I would never have gone out with you if I'd known—if I'd suspected——'

'No?' Mike sounded sceptical. 'Come on, Shelley, we both know how ambitious you were!

Good God, everyone at the station knew you were determined to make it, one way or the other. And—well, I'll admit it—I was only too happy to go along. We were good together, Shelley. We can be good again——'

'No! *No*!'

'If you keep on saying no, Shelley, you're going to force me to *make* you believe it. For Christ's sake, Lesley's death was a shock to me, too. But it was nothing for you to get so steamed up about. I mean—you hardly knew the woman.'

Shelley trembled, as memories of the whole sordid affair swept over her again. Of course she had been upset about it. There were times when she had almost convinced herself that Lesley Berlitz's death had been a direct result of her own selfishness, a cross she was being made to bear for the recklessness of becoming involved with a married man. The fact that as soon as she had learned that Mike was not in the process of divorcing his wife, that Lesley was, in fact, a major shareholder in the television station, and Mike had no intention of jeopardising his position by seeking a separation, Shelley had broken off their relationship, was harder to believe—particularly as Mike had continued to pursue her as energetically as before. But, so long as Lesley was alive, Shelley had been able to cope with that. His wife's death from cancer, some twenty months later, had brought the situation to a head, and the subsequent drain on Shelley's mental resources had caused the virtual breakdown of her nervous system.

'I don't think there's any point in continuing this conversation,' Shelley said now, her knuckles almost as white as the receiver she was holding. 'I had hoped my—my absence would make you see the truth of what I've been trying to tell you for the past three months, but evidently it hasn't. I'm sorry. But there's nothing I can do about it——'

'Like hell!' Mike lost his temper. 'You listen to me, Shelley: I won't take this, do you hear? I don't care what some over-priced psychiatrist has been telling you. I don't care if your conscience won't let you accept what you know is true. We belong together, and I'm going to see we stay together. Goddammit, you belong to me!'

Shelley replaced the receiver she was holding with a distinct little click, starting seconds later when the phone gave an unexpected little ping. But it reminded her that Mike could easily dial her number again, and after a moment's consideration, she lifted the receiver off the rest again, and laid it down beside the phone on the bedside table. Then, after giving herself a few moments to recover, she got determinedly to her feet and walked back to her own room.

Realising there was no chance of her being able to rest with the knowledge of Mike's call to disturb her, Shelley decided to get dressed. A cool shower and two of her tablets—which she noticed were getting rather low—made her feel slightly more human, and ignoring the pounding in her head, she went downstairs.

Breaking one of her own rules, she went to find Marsha in her studio. Until now, she had refrained from disturbing her friend, whatever the provocation, but in this instance, she knew she *had* to talk to somebody.

One look at the younger woman's pale face was enough to convince Marsha that something was seriously wrong, and abandoning her painting, she came quickly to meet her.

'My dear—what is it?' she exclaimed, gazing

anxiously into Shelley's bruised green eyes, and Shelley shook her head dazedly before seeking the support of a wooden chair.

'Mike rang,' she said bleakly, allowing her slim wrists to hang weakly over the arms. 'I'm sorry. I just had to tell someone.'

Marsha moistened her lips and then, realising she was still holding her paintbrush, she quickly disposed of it. 'How did he know where you were?' she asked, coming back to kneel by Shelley's chair, and Shelley gave a helpless shrug before making a response.

'He guessed, and then used his influence to get the 'phone number,' she responded flatly. 'I told him our relationship was over, but he wouldn't listen.'

Marsha frowned. 'You mean—he doesn't accept it?'

'No. He doesn't accept it,' agreed Shelley, repeating her words parrot-fashion. 'Oh, Marsha, what am I going to do? I can't go back to that, I just can't!'

Hearing the rising note of hysteria in Shelley's voice, Marsha endeavoured to calm her. 'You don't have to go back,' she declared, taking the girl's hand in both of hers and squeezing it reassuringly. 'Darling, have you forgotten? There are weeks and weeks before you need even *think* about going back to London!'

'But sooner or later——'

'Sooner or later, Mike Berlitz will get off your back,' declared Marsha firmly. 'He'll get the message. Just don't give in to him.'

Shelley shook her head. 'You don't understand.'

'What don't I understand?'

'Marsha, he's my boss! He practically owns the television station!'

'No one practically *owns* a television station,' declared Marsha convincingly. 'Shelley, the man's persistent, I'll give you that. But if he's threatening you with losing your job——'

'He's not threatening me,' said Shelley wearily. 'At least, not with losing my job, anyway.' To her relief, the panic inside her was beginning to respond to Marsha's calming influence. 'He just won't accept that I don't love him. And right now, I don't know if I can handle that.'

'Then stay here until you can,' said Marsha reasonably. 'Now that Dickon is getting married, I don't have any other commitments.'

'Oh, Marsha——' Shelley closed her eyes against the unpalatable reminder of her own deceit. It seemed that whichever way she turned, she was faced with problems of her own making. Perhaps she ought seriously to consider an alternative solution; one where Mike, and Marsha, and most particularly, Ben, would not be hurt by her destructive personality. 'I—thanks, but no thanks,' she murmured unhappily, withdrawing her hand from Marsha's grasp, gently, but firmly. 'You're sweet, but I can't take advantage of your kindness. I—I've got to deal with this myself. In my own way.'

'Well—just so long as you remember Dickon and I are behind you, every inch of the way,' said Marsha staunchly, and Shelley despised herself anew for getting involved in their lives.

During the following week, Shelley made a determined effort to put the past behind her—a past that contained not only Mike, but Ben, too. Both relationships were doomed to failure, and if she wanted to make a successful future for herself, she had to stop looking over her shoulder.

All the same, it wasn't easy trying to behave as if Marsha's support was all she needed, and her small supply of capsules dwindled alarmingly. Dr Lanyard had said she should only take the capsules if the headaches became unbearable, but lately she seemed seldom to be without one. In addition to which, she found the analgesic quality of the drug helped to keep her brain less active, and in consequence she was forced to consult Marsha about the possibilities of renewing her prescription.

'Why don't you go and see Charles?' suggested Marsha at once, but Shelley was not enthusiastic.

'I don't want to discuss my physical weaknesses with him, Marsha,' she protested unhappily. 'I'd prefer to speak to a stranger; someone without any preconceived ideas about my way of life.'

'Mmm.' Marsha was not entirely unsympathetic to her point of view. 'It would have to be a doctor in Low Burton then. I'll ask Charles. He might know someone.'

'I'd rather you didn't.' Shelley gave her a rueful smile. 'Honestly, Marsha, I'd prefer to make my own arrangements. The fewer people who know what a wreck I am, the better.'

'Oh, Shelley!' Marsha sighed. 'You're not a wreck. You're just having a difficult time, that's all. Look—why don't you ask Dickon? He's bound to know who to recommend and who not.'

Faced with this second alternative, Shelley felt obliged to concede. She had no good reason for refusing, and besides, it might bring Ben to his senses to learn that she was far from the untarnished innocence of youth.

'I've made you an appointment with a Dr Sheridan,' Marsha remarked the following afternoon, when Shelley returned from a visit to the village. 'Dickon says he's the most experienced of the doctors in the practice, so I made the appointment for tomorrow morning at ten.'

Shelley moistened her lips. 'Ben—I mean, *Dickon's* been here?'

'No. I rang him,' said Marsha airily. 'I waited for you to do it, and when you didn't I did.'

'I see.' Shelley forced a smile. 'Well—thanks. I—I was waiting until he came out here.'

'I shouldn't hold your breath,' commented Marsha drily. 'So long as Jennifer's father is so ill, Dickon's not going to have a lot of free time. And I suppose it's only natural that he should want to spend what he has with her.'

Shelley hesitated. 'Did he say that?'

'More or less.' Marsha grimaced. 'I don't know. Dickon seems different somehow. I'd have thought, with you being here, he'd have done his damndest to spend some time with us. Heavens, before you came, he could talk of nothing else.' She paused, regarding her friend with sudden inspiration: 'You haven't—I mean, you and Dickon haven't had a row or anything, have you? If you have, I wish you'd tell me. It's just not like him to be so—distant.'

'Of course not.' Shelley's answer was automatic, and to her relief Marsha accepted it without demur.

'I didn't really think you had,' she admitted gloomily.'Nothing is ever that simple. You don't think—well, I have wondered if he and Jennifer are having problems he doesn't want to tell me about. I did give the idea that she might be pregnant some consideration, but surely Dickon would know that I'd never reproach him for that.' She pulled a wry face. 'Good Lord, I'd be delighted. Even if I would have to abandon all my plans for a white wedding.'

Shelley's nails dug into her palms as she turned away. Knowing what she did, the idea that Jennifer might be pregnant seemed an unlikely solution for Ben's absence. But it did promote another disturbing notion. Although she had not thought of it at the time, she had taken no precautions when she and Ben had made love, and she knew he had been in no mood to care. Indeed, remembering that interlude, with all its unrestrained passion, she doubted if either of them could have made that choice even had they wanted to.

Involuntarily, her hand strayed to the quivering flatness of her stomach. It was possible, she supposed, though highly unlikely in her present condition. But, nevertheless, it was proof of her weakness in her dealings with Ben, and a salutary reminder of a more physical vulnerability.

'What do you think?'

Realising Marsha was looking at her rather doubtfully now, Shelley quickly thrust her hands behind her back. 'Oh—I think you're probably being too sensitive,' she murmured, reaching for a magazine. 'I—er—how old is this Dr Sheridan? Did—did Dickon say?'

Marsha shrugged. 'No. But as he's the senior partner I imagine he'll be in his sixties, at least.' She made an effort to put her own problems aside, and smiled. 'He'll probably tell you that what you need is a husband and a handful of children to worry about.' Her eyes twinkled. 'Which isn't such a bad idea, when I come to think of it.'

In fact, Dr Sheridan was not as old as Marsha had predicted. Shelley gauged his age to be somewhere in his middle fifties, and he wasn't half as old fashioned as she had anticipated.

'I suppose you're used to being told that a woman isn't cut out to be a high-powered executive, aren't you?' he remarked, after giving her a brief examination. 'But, believe me, I get just as many business *men* coming in here, suffering from the effects of hypertension. We used to call it overwork in my young day, or high blood-pressure, if the patient looked apoplectic.'

'But—I don't have high blood pressure, do I?' protested Shelley in some alarm, and the physician smiled as he put his stethoscope away.

'No,' he said firmly. 'I think I can reassure you on that score. You're too pale, of course, and you need to put on at least seven pounds in weight, but apart from the headaches you mention, you're in fairly good shape. Physically, at least.'

'Thank you.' Shelley was relieved.

'So——' He arched an eyebrow and regarded her encouragingly. 'Do you want to tell me what caused them to start?'

'I'd rather not.' Shelley bent her head. 'Something happened that—that I couldn't cope with. I just collapsed one day at work. My doctor called it a—a trial breakdown.'

'I see.' Dr Sheridan nodde. 'Well, I suggest you try and avoid the kind of situation that creates these headaches. You say they've persisted—even though there's presumably no reason for them now?'

'Not exactly.' Shelley could feel the warm colour entering her cheeks as she endeavoured to sidestep his question. 'Oh—really, I'm feeling much better; honestly. If you could just repeat the prescription, I shan't bother you again.'

The doctor agreed, but reluctantly Shelley knew, and as she emerged from the surgery into the cool chill of the damp morning, she suspected he would be getting in touch with her own doctor to inform him of the situation.

A Land-Rover overtook her as she walked towards the market square and the chemist's shop she had seen there. Its grey lines did not make it in any way distinguishable from any other Land-Rover, but Shelley could tell from the prickling of her flesh that it was Ben's. It was hardly any surprise when it didn't slow or stop, and she walked on determinedly, ignoring the hollow feeling in her stomach.

When she reached the square, however, she found the vehicle in question parked outside the pharmacy, and she thought what bad luck it was that he should have business there at the same time she did.

But Ben was not in the chemist's shop. When Shelley came abreast of the Land-Rover she discovered he was still seated behind the wheel, though he thrust open his door and slid out to confront her.

'What's wrong?' he asked abruptly, and Shelley stared at him blankly, too shocked to respond. It was so good to see him again, however she might deny it, and her eyes moved hungrily over his lean frame, severely encased in black roll-necked sweater and matching jeans. 'You went to see Sheridan,' he reminded her, nodding towards the folded prescription she was clenching in one hand. 'Are you ill?'

'Oh——' Shelley managed to drag her scattered senses together and shook her head. 'I—no. No, I just went to get something for—for a headache. How are you? Still working overtime, I suppose.'

'What's that supposed to mean?'

Ben was aggressive, and she could hardly blame him. After all, they had hardly parted on the best of terms, and she had not forgotten his anger on that occasion.

'Your mother says you've had very little free time,' she replied now, carefully. 'What with Jennifer's father being ill, and——'

'We've got a replacement,' Ben cut in coldly. 'Dennis Armitage. I believe I mentioned him to you. He's given up his holiday to help out.'

'Oh! Oh, I see.' Shelley put up a hand to her head, feeling the dampening strands of hair that had freed themselves from the knot clinging to her neck. 'Well—I'm sure your mother will be relieved.'

'But not you,' Ben inserted harshly. 'Evidently I'm responsible for your feeling out of sorts. Or at least that's what my mother thinks.' His lips twisted mockingly. 'What have you been telling her?'

'Nothing!' Shelley almost choked on the word. 'What do you mean? What has Marsha been saying? I've never mentioned you.'

'Oh, I can believe it.' Ben expelled his breath heavily. 'Nevertheless, my mother wants me to show you a little more—courtesy. You're fond of me—or so she says—and I haven't shown you the consideration I should.'

'Oh, Ben!' Shelley gazed at him helplessly, and Ben tore his eyes away to stare broodingly at the toes of his boots.

'She says Berlitz has been making a nuisance of himself again, and I'm to provide a distraction,' he continued doggedly. 'I told her I was sure you wouldn't agree with her, but she wouldn't listen to me. So here I am.' He lifted his head. 'What do you want to do about it?'

Shelley frowned. 'You mean—your mother asked you to meet me here?'

'No.' Ben's jaw tightened. 'She asked me to come out to the house this afternoon. Only I preferred to gauge your reaction in private.'

'This is hardly private!' Shelley gestured unsteadily about her. 'Anyone can see us.'

'And that bothers you?'

'It should bother you!'

'Why?' The silvery eyes were slivers of ice. 'To all intents and purposes, we met by accident. What are you afraid of?' His eyes darkened. 'I'm not Mike Berlitz!'

'What do you mean?'

'I mean, I won't force myself upon you,' retorted Ben grimly. 'It seems like you told my mother a different story to the one you told me. But don't worry. You told me how you felt about me, I'm not about to argue with that. Just tell me to go and I'll go.'

'Ben——'

'Yes?' He propped his hips against the body of the Land-Rover and folded his arms. 'I know—my mother got it wrong. You don't want to see me, either. I guessed as much.'

'That's not true.' Shelley moved her head despairingly from side to side, but Ben was not convinced.

'How was it you put it?—When we were making love, you felt more like my mother than my mistress!'

'Ben!' Shelley caught her breath. 'I didn't say that!'

'That's what it sounded like to me.' Ben pushed himself away from the Land-Rover and shrugged his broad shoulders. 'Okay. So I'm wrong again. So what's new?'

Shelley sighed. 'Ben, please! I just don't want to hurt you.'

'Don't you mean—hurt yourself?' he enquired roughly, and without seeming able to prevent herself she grasped his arm.

The muscled strength of his forearm was taut

beneath her fingers, the heat of his skin reaching through the shetland wool to warm her rain-chilled fingers. She knew she shouldn't have touched him—that she had no right to touch him—but she held on to him anyway, looking up into his hard young face.

'I'm trying to be sensible about this,' she exclaimed fiercely, resisting the impulse to push the damp swathe of rain-darkened hair back from his forehead. 'I'm trying to do the right thing. You're not free, Ben. You're engaged to be married to a girl of your own age and your own type. You just find me a—a novelty, that's all. The archetypal older woman, who you found painfully easy to seduce!'

The bitterness she felt as she said these last words caused a grimace of self-derision to cross her face. She could imagine Mike's contempt if he ever learned of her infatuation for a younger man. Once he had recovered from his anger, he would probably regard it as rough justice, the kind of retribution deserved by someone who contravened his wishes.

'You—are crazy!' retorted Ben unsteadily, gazing at her with eyes suddenly molten with emotion. 'I told you once before—I wanted you when I was eighteen, only I never thought you'd look at me then. But, you came here, and as soon as I saw you again—for Christ's sake, Shelley, I'm in love with you! And I don't give a damn how old you are!'

Shelley's breathing felt constricted. 'Ben—you don't know what you're saying——'

'Of course I know what I'm saying,' he interrupted her harshly. 'I'm saying I want you—and I need you—and that without you, life doesn't seem to have much meaning.'

'Oh, Ben!' Shelley was trembling now, and uncaring of who might see them, Ben put one arm about her shoulders, sliding his fingers beneath her chin and tipping her face to his.

'Let's go to my house,' he said, his thumb probing the delicate contours of her ear. 'After all, it's what my mother wanted: that we should spend some time together.'

But not like this, thought Shelley despairingly, his warm breath fanning her cheek. With an effort, she drew away from him. 'I—I've got to get this prescription filled,' she stammered, stepping past him into the doorway of the chemist's, and with a careless shrug he followed her, into the lighted brilliance of the shop.

While the pharmacist measured out the number of capsules, he chatted away to Ben, who was evidently well known in Low Burton. As it was a country area, Shelley supposed most people had a pet of some sort, or were involved with animals through their work. On top of which, Ben's personality was such that he would be popular in any community, and it was obvious he enjoyed the familiarity. But how popular would he be if he jilted his fiancée, particularly at a time when her father was so ill? Would these people forgive him if he abandoned Jennifer Chater and took his mother's best friend as his wife?

CHAPTER EIGHT

SHELLEY entered Ben's house with some misgivings. No matter what he said, it didn't seem right that she should be there, and when he turned to shut the door behind them, she walked quickly along the narrow passage and into the living room.

With the rain pattering at the windows now, the house had acquired an air of intimacy it had not previously possessed, and it was impossible not to imagine how cosy it would be on a winter's evening, with the curtains drawn and a log fire burning in the open hearth. She could even see herself curled up on the rug in front of the blaze, her shoulders pressed against Ben's knees, his hand resting on her shoulder . . .

The elusive trend of her thoughts was seductive, and when Ben's arms slid around her from behind, she yielded against him, almost with relief. But when his mouth sought the tempting curve of her nape while his hands probed the studded fastening of her leather jacket, she came abruptly to her senses.

'We can't do this, Ben,' she protested huskily, pulling herself away from him. She shook her head. 'I can't hurt Marsha, and you can't leave Jennifer.'

Ben's face took on a weary expression. 'I thought we'd dealt with that.'

Shelley sighed. 'Just because I—just because *we*—might want one another, doesn't mean we can just walk roughshod over everyone else's feelings.'

'What about our feelings?' enquired Ben

bitterly. 'You do *have* feelings, I assume. Or was that little fiasco outside Hobson's simply intended to avoid a scene?'

Shelley's lips twisted. 'You know it wasn't.'

'Do I?'

'Yes. Oh—*yes*!' With a gesture of defeat, Shelley abandoned the argument for the present, crossing the space she had created between them and sliding her arms around his neck. 'I have feelings,' she admitted unsteadily, pulling his mouth to hers, and with a groan of satisfaction, Ben submitted to her demands.

It was an unfamiliar delight to slide her fingers into the rain-slick vitality of his hair, and to stroke his neck where it disappeared inside the collar of his sweater. His flesh was so smooth, and yet so different from her own, the muscles that jerked beneath the skin evidence of the physical effect she had upon him. His lips parted to the eager caress of hers, welcoming her tongue into his mouth with disarming innocence. But when she would have withdrawn it again, the tenor of their embrace changed, and the initiator became the initiated as Ben made his own assault on her senses.

The leather jerkin fell heedlessly to the floor as his hands found the buttons of the green silk shirt beneath. For once, Shelley was not wearing a bra, discarding the item when she had anticipated the doctor would require to give her an examination, and Ben's fingers trembled as they closed about her breasts.

Shelley would have closed her eyes against the look of possession in his eyes as he massaged the swollen peaks, but Ben would not let her. With his mouth taking on a very sensual curve, he held her gaze as his thumbs brought the honey-brown nipples to pulsating life. Then, her breath quickening helplessly, she watched as he lowered his head to suckle first at one breast, then at the other, his tongue tugging wetly at each eager offering.

As he drew back, her eyes were drawn, almost against her will, to the revealing tautness of his pants, and he took both her hands and drew her insistently towards the low sofa.

'Ought—oughtn't we to go upstairs?' she breathed huskily, as he tugged her down on to his lap and she felt the unmistakable maleness of his body, but Ben only shook his head.

'I don't want to go upstairs,' he murmured, nuzzling the unfastened shirt from her shoulder, and Shelley felt incapable of denying him anything.

With a rapid movement, he pulled off his own sweater, and then lowered her on to the sofa beside him. Crushing her softness beneath the muscled hardness of his chest, he covered her yielding body with his, and then the hungry possession of his tongue was in her mouth. With his hands sliding down to probe her thigh, quivering beneath the thin cotton of her pants, it was incredibly difficult to remember this was Marsha's son, and the difference in their ages seemed unworthy of consideration when he could so easily arouse her deepest emotions.

Abandoning her conscience, Shelley gave in to the demands he was making on her, and as he continued to drug her senses with long, soul-inflaming kisses, her hands began their own exploration. From the rippling muscles of his shoulders, she found the hollowing curve of his spine and then, baulked by the waistband of his pants, she transferred her attention to his chest. His nipples were button-hard beneath her fingertips, and the fine dark hair that moved with such sensual abrasion against her breasts tickled her palms. But when her hands moved lower, and found the swollen shaft of his manhood throbbing beneath the cloth, he shuddered violently and rolled to one side to unbuckle his belt.

'Let me,' said Shelley unsteadily, pushing his hands away and releasing the zip, and presently he was able to kick his pants aside.

Without a trace of prudishness, Ben straddled her now, loosening her pants and pressing them down over her hips. He followed their progress with his lips, allowing his tongue to stroke sensuously across the flatness of her stomach, and after making a cursory examination of her navel, he reached the quivering cluster of red-gold curls that marked her femininity.

'Ben!' she protested weakly, jerking beneath his probing fingers, and Ben made a ruefully amused sound as he rubbed his face against her, reluctant to leave her sweetness, and then the needs of his own body overwhelmed his failing restraint.

Parting her legs, he moved between them, and feeling the heat of him entering her, possessing her, filling her with the memory of how good it had been before, Shelley's legs clutched him convulsively to her. She had spent too long refusing to acknowledge how much she wanted him, but now, with his hands beneath her hips, with his tongue plundering her mouth, and the pulsating length of him buried deep within her, she could give in to the needs and desires she had been stifling. Her nails raked his shoulders as he thrust and thrust against her, her little cries and moans reaching a crescendo as she arched herself towards him to meet his plunging rhythm.

It was like that other time, only better. The

ordinary things of life—age, experience, identity—
were all consumed by the raging fire of their
passion, and when the precipice was reached they
were not two beings, but one. For seconds in time
they hung, suspended, drained of all emotion, yet
aware of the incredible unity they had achieved.
Then, Ben slumped across her, his sweat-
moistened body relaxed in her arms ...

She thought he was asleep, but he wasn't, and
when she tried to move, his lids lifted to allow him
to survey her with lazily sated eyes. 'Now tell me
we don't belong together,' he taunted softly, his
thumb probing the vulnerable curve of her mouth,
and she parted her teeth deliberately and bit the
teasing pad.

'Ouch,' he protested indignantly, pulling the
injured digit away, and she wound her legs and
arms around him in sensual abandon.

'All right,' she said, ignoring any lingering shred
of conscience and meeting his gaze with unguarded
eyes. 'I admit it. We do need one another. And—
and although I don't want to hurt anyone, maybe
we can work something out.'

'I know it!' said Ben fiercely, cradling her face
between his palms and rubbing his lips sensuously
over hers. 'I'll tell my mother today. It's only
fair——'

'No!'

Shelley's swift denial cut into his words, and
Ben drew back to rest on his knees, regarding her
with a sudden lack of comprehension. 'No?' he
echoed slowly. 'But, you just said——'

'I said we needed one another,' said Shelley
quietly, his withdrawal enabling her to lever herself
up on her elbows. 'We do. I'm not denying it. But
that's not to say we should destroy the happiness
of the people we love.'

A scowl took the place of Ben's earlier jubilation. 'For Christ's sake, Shelley——'

'Listen to me!' Shelley managed to shift back from him, drawing up her legs to shield her body, needing the small protection to give her the strength to go on. 'Ben, I know what I'm talking about, believe me. I know you want me. I know that when we're—together—it's really good. But it's not enough——'

'What do you mean, it's not enough?'

'I don't love you, Ben. I like you. I really like you. And I'm attracted to you, I'm not denying that. But anything else——'

Ben's jaw hardened. 'So what are you saying?'

'I'm saying——' Shelley hesitated, choosing her words with care '—that we should enjoy what we have——'

'Like this, you mean?' Ben's lips twisted. 'A furtive little hole-in-the-corner affair, like you had with Mike Berlitz?'

Shelley's face burned. 'I did not have a—a hole-in-the-corner affair with Mike Berlitz!'

'What would you call it then? You knew that he was married!'

'I did not. At least——' Shelley struggled to defend herself, 'I believed he was getting a divorce.'

'Oh, really.'

'Yes, really!' Shelley stared at him in horror. 'Don't you believe me?'

'Berlitz seems to think you knew,' retorted Ben savagely. 'He believes that your ambition conveniently blinded you to the real facts of the affair. That you'd have done anything to claw your way to your present position!'

Shelley trembled. 'How—how do you know that?' She fought against the obvious explanation, but she had to ask: 'Is that what your mother thinks?'

'No!' Ben's response was too instinctive to be a lie. 'Then—how——'

'Sarah overheard a conversation you had with Berlitz,' retorted Ben wearily, pushing himself up from the sofa and reaching for his pants.

'Sarah!'

Shelley was stunned, and Ben made a rather rueful gesture. 'Beggars can't be choosers,' he said, picking up his sweater. 'I was desperate for news of you—and she supplied it.'

'When?' Shelley gazed at him with eyes dark with the suspicion of his betrayal. 'Did you ask her about me?'

'No. No.' Ben expelled his breath heavily. 'For God's sake, don't look at me like that. I didn't believe it.'

'Until now,' put in Shelley bitterly, dragging a cushion in front of her for protection, and stumbling off the sofa. 'My God! Conflict does create strange bedfellows, doesn't it?'

'Sarah is not a bedfellow!' grated Ben angrily. 'I met her in town. What she told me was said in all innocence!'

'Oh, come on, Ben!'

'It's true. She didn't come right out and say you were an ambitious bitch with amoral leanings. That's my interpretation!'

'Is it?' Shelley was shaking so much, she couldn't even fasten the button at her waist, and with a groan of remorse, Ben thrust her hands aside and did it for her.

Then, unable to resist the urge to dispel the wounded pallor from her cheeks, he drew her protesting body towards him. 'I don't mean it,' he said, in a shaken voice. 'God knows, I don't know what I'm saying! I love you. *I love you.* Don't you know I'm only hurting you because you're tearing me to pieces?'

Shelley tried to fight him, but what he had said had shocked her to the core, and weakness was no shield to feelings too raw to be disguised. When he kissed her, she kissed him back, her hands clinging to the nape of his neck, and his fingers slid possessively into her hair, as her lips opened eagerly to his.

'Okay,' he said, at last, just as she was about to make her confession. 'We'll do it your way. I won't tell my mother or Jennifer. But don't imagine it will be easy, because it won't.'

'Ben——'

'No. Don't say anything else,' he silenced her tautly. 'I don't think I can take any more right now. Get dressed, and I'll take you back to where you left your car. You can tell my mother we met in town and that I—offered you a drink or something. That way you've covered yourself in case anyone saw us come in here together.'

'Oh, Ben——'

'Get dressed!' he repeated flatly, striding towards the door. 'I've got to phone Armitage. I shouldn't be more than a couple of minutes.'

'So you saw Dickon's house,' said Marsha with satisfaction, passing Shelley a dish of salad. 'Did he show you around? Did you see the kitchen?'

'I—saw a little of it, yes,' murmured Shelley unhappily, helping herself to a slice of tomato. 'I like the view at the back. The river makes it marvellously private.'

'Yes, doesn't it?' Marsha smiled. 'And although it's not a new house, the previous owner made it over completely. It's really modern, and ideal for a single person.'

Shelley moistened her lips. 'I imagine a couple could manage there quite well,' she ventured cautiously. 'I doubt if—if Dickon will want the expense of a new house, immediately after the expense of a wedding.'

'Oh—I think I might help out there,' remarked Marsha confidently. 'A new house might make an ideal wedding gift, and then Dickon could sell the old one and keep the money as a nest-egg for when the babies start to come along.'

Shelley hid a wince, and tried to apply herself with some enthusiasm to the home-baked ham on her plate. 'You could be right,' she managed, forking a square of meat into her mouth. 'It seems a shame though. The house in Ditchburn Lane is very—cosy.'

'Then why don't you buy it?' suggested Marsha, with the air of someone who has achieved her objective, and Shelley sighed.

'Marsha——'

'Well, why not? Oh, I'm not suggesting you should give up your flat in London, or anything like that. I simply think it would be a good idea if you had somewhere of your own, far from the vindictive demands of men like Mike Berlitz!'

'Marsha, I don't need a house——'

'Everyone needs a house,' retorted Marsha, undeterred. 'Oh, a flat is all very well, but it's not like owning a whole property, with a garden and everything. I've seen you helping Martin about the place. I bet an occupation like gardening is exactly what you need.'

'You'll be telling me next that all I really need is a home and family,' said Shelley impatiently, and then bent her head when Marsha fixed her eyes upon her.

'Well, I must admit, you don't seem to be enjoying the cut and thrust of television,' she responded drily. 'If you were half as tough as you like to think you are, Mike Berlitz would never be able to get to you like he does. But you're not. You're too sensitive, Shelley. Compared to those hyenas, you're as helpless as a kid!'

'Don't you mean a goat?' enquired Shelley wearily, knowing she was right, but unwilling to admit what it might mean. Then, as Sarah came to collect their plates, she met the maid's insolent stare with some determination. 'There are predators everywhere, if you choose to look for them,' she added, watching the look of uncertainty that entered the girl's eyes. 'Don't imagine London has cornered the market. Why, you never know who might be waiting to put a knife in your back.'

Marsha looked at her strangely. 'That was said with some feeling. What has Dickon been saying to you?'

'Dickon?' Shelley expelled her breath as Sarah hurriedly left the room. 'I don't believe his name was mentioned.'

'No, but—well, you spoke with such vehemence, you must have meant somebody. You surely don't think I——'

'No. No, of course not.' Shelley realised she had to make some sort of explanation and sighed. 'Oh, if you must know, I think Sarah listened in to that call I got from Mike. The—er—the 'phone pinged—you know; like it does when someone's put down the extension. And she was the only likely suspect.'

'I see.' Marsha whistled through her teeth. 'Why didn't you tell me straight away?'

'Oh——' Shelley could hardly explain that until Ben had brought it up, she had thought nothing of the betraying sound. 'I—er—you know how upset I was when Mike 'phoned. I suppose I forgot all about it.'

Marsha frowned. 'That girl really will have to go——'

'Oh, no!'

'Oh, yes.' Marsha was determined. 'I won't have her eavesdropping on conversations and listening in to calls. It's not the first time it's happened. And she's far too familiar, as I've said before. Mrs Braid's niece is looking for work. I'll ask her if she'd be interested in taking over Sarah's duties. She's a much nicer woman, and she's at least ten years older.'

'Oh, Marsha! I wouldn't have told you if I'd known you'd be likely to fire the girl! I'll speak to her myself. Really! I'd rather.'

'I'm sorry, Shelley, but you've given me the excuse I've been looking for.' Marsha was adamant. 'Now, please—don't give it another thought. I shan't tell her what you've told me. I'll just say that her behaviour has come to my notice, and leave it at that. She won't know who to blame. She'll probably think Mrs Carr has been spying on her.'

Shelley would have protested further, but the sound of the telephone interrupted them. 'Damn! Right in the middle of lunch,' exclaimed Marsha aggravatedly; but she went to answer it anyway, and Shelley suspected she was glad of the diversion.

Marsha's face was flushed when she came back, and Shelley looked up at her half-apprehensively. It wasn't like Marsha to get so excited about anything, and for a heart-stopping moment, Shelley wondered if her involvement with Ben had been exposed.

'You'll never guess what's happened!' she exclaimed, and still wary of the explanation, Shelley shook her head. 'They're going to do a television special, all about my work,' declared Marsha excitedly. 'Can you believe it? A full hour's programme about me and my paintings. That was Tim Hedley. He's going to produce it.'

'Tim Hedley!' echoed Shelley faintly, recognising the name of Capitol Television's senior arts producer. 'I can hardly believe it.'

'Nor could I,' Marsha added incredulously. 'He wants me to go down to London next week for discussions about the format. He's suggested I spend the night at an hotel—they're paying, of course—and that way we'll have a good twenty-four hours to come up with a satisfactory profile. What do you think?'

What did she think? Shelley moistened her lips. In all honesty, she was delighted for Marsha's sake, but she couldn't help the unwilling suspicion that Mike was behind it. She couldn't see what he had to gain by giving Marsha some well-deserved publicity, but it seemed more than a coincidence that the offer should be made at this time.

'I think you should do it,' she said now, refusing to allow her doubts to dampen Marsha's excitement. 'Really. I think it's long overdue. They'll be asking you to chair your own chat-show next.' She forced a smile. 'You know—*Master Class with Manning!* Or *Art for Artisans!*'

'Oh—you!' Marsha was as excited as a girl, and Shelley prayed this was not some clever trick on Mike's part to get her to do what he wanted. 'You don't mind if I go away for a couple of days, do you? I mean—you will be all right here on your own?'

'Of course I'll be all right.' Shelley was quick to

put her mind at rest, but as if the younger woman's innocent expression was *too* happy, *too* enthusiastic, Marsha came abruptly back to earth.

'You don't think Mike Berlitz is behind this, do you?' she ventured, watching Shelley's face intently, and it took all her ingenuity not to reveal her own uncertainty.

'Now, why should he be?' she demanded, infusing her voice with exactly the right mixture of reason and logic. 'What could Mike possibly have to gain by offering you this chance? No.' Shelley shook her head. 'It may be that speaking to me reminded him what a marvellous opportunity he was missing.'

'You're awfully good for my ego, do you know that?' exclaimed Marsha at once, but it was obvious Shelley's words had reassured her. 'Well—if you're sure.' She shook her head. 'Provisionally we've arranged it for next Tuesday and Wednesday.'

Ben arrived, unexpectedly, the following afternoon. For once, Jennifer was with him, and Shelley had to steel herself to face the younger girl's too-knowing eyes.

'Oh, Daddy's much better,' she replied, in response to Marsha's immediate enquiry. 'The doctor says he's out of danger at last, and we're hoping to get him home again at the end of next week.'

'That is good news.'

Marsha was genuinely delighted, and Shelley offered her own good wishes for his complete recovery. As Ben had predicted, it was not easy to speak to Jennifer as if everything was just as before, and she despised herself utterly for the weakness that had forced her into such an intolerable position. How could she do this? she asked herself. How could she stand here, mouthing platitudes, when if Jennifer knew the truth, she would want to scratch her eyes out? And how could she go on with the deception, when by doing so she was destroying her self-respect?

It wasn't too difficult to find reasons. They were there in plenty. Reasons why she was deceiving Jennifer and betraying Marsha's trust. And they still sounded quite convincing when she compared them to the alternatives. But they acquired a distinctly hollow resonance when she was faced with the real victim of her treachery, and she wondered then if anything was worth such an unholy sacrifice.

Yet, she argued, wasn't it better for Jennifer not to know of Ben's infatuation? What would Marsha gain from learning of her son's obsession? Soon, when she went back to London, he would forget all about her. It was amazing how often distance achieved what proximity could not. What was the point of allowing Ben to break his engagement, just to satisfy some misguided notion of honesty? This way, no one would be hurt. Except, of course, herself—which was only justice, after all.

Even so, and in spite of all her resolution, nothing could prevent the uncontrollable surge of emotion Shelley felt upon seeing Ben again. He came into the living room behind his fiancée, pushing back his sun-bleached hair with a careless hand, his cream silk shirt opened down his chest to expose the muscular beauty of his body. Just the sight of him caused a wave of heat to engulf her, and even the coolness of a halter top and Bermudas could not prevent the hollows of her body from pooling with sweat.

If she had been afraid that he might look at her in a certain way, or cause her any embarrassment, she was soon disabused of the notion. On the contrary, apart from a fleeting appraisal on his arrival, with eyes that held nothing but a polite detachment, Ben showed little interest in her presence, supplementing his fiancée's news of her father with casual comments of his own.

Inevitably, the conversation moved to Marsha's exciting offer, and Shelley soon realised that her friend had already broken the news to her son. 'You must be really flattered,' said Jennifer, with her usual lack of tact. 'Did Shelley fix it up for you? That's the television company she works for, isn't it?'

Marsha exchanged a rueful grimace with her friend, and then gave Jennifer a generous smile. 'Would you believe they actually made an independent offer?' she asked drily. 'There are one or two people around who really think I've got some talent!'

Jennifer coloured prettily. 'Oh, you know me,' she exclaimed, as Ben gave her an impatient look. 'I didn't mean your pictures weren't clever, or anything. I just thought it was an obvious coincidence.'

'Think nothing of it,' said Marsha, getting up from the sofa. 'I'll go and organise some tea. Dickon, will you come and help me? It's Mrs Braid's afternoon off, and I don't like to trouble Mrs Carr.'

Shelley wished Marsha had asked her, but it seemed obvious she wanted a private word with her son. Shelley hoped it was not to do with Sarah. Since hearing of the television special, Marsha had said no more about dismissing the girl, and Shelley was hoping she might dissuade her. She didn't want Sarah's disappointment to add to all her other sins, and she felt sure that given time Marsha would relent.

'Are you still enjoying your holiday?'

Jennifer's wooden enquiry broke into her thoughts, and Shelley realised belatedly how rude her prolonged silence must have seemed. 'I'm sorry,' she said, contriving a polite smile. 'I—yes.

Yes, I'm enjoying my stay very much. It's such a pleasant change from the city.'

'Hmm.' Jennifer did not look convinced. 'I'd have thought you'd be climbing the walls by now. Craygill is okay, but you must admit, it is boring.'

'I've not been bored,' said Shelley honestly, and Jennifer nodded her head.

'No,' she said tersely. 'I understand you've been getting Ben to show you around. He doesn't really have the time, you know. Only he's too polite to tell you.'

Shelley took a deep breath. 'I don't think I've been taking up too much of your fiancé's time,' she replied carefully. 'As a matter of fact, his mother and I have seen very little of him since your father was taken ill.'

'But you did waste a whole morning yesterday with him, didn't you?' retorted Jennifer, evidently getting into her stride. 'And people will start talking if you don't leave him alone.

Shelley caught her lower lip between her teeth. 'I don't think you have anything to worry about, Jennifer——'

'Oh, I know that!' The girl was contemptuous now. 'Ben's not the type to be interested in a middle-aged woman! But he does admire your work, and I suppose he's flattered, too, that you seem to find him so attractive!'

Shelley was speechless. A middle-aged woman indeed! Well, perhaps that's how she appeared to Jennifer, she thought ruefully. After all, when she had been Jennifer's age, anyone over thirty had seemed to have one foot in the grave.

Before she could fashion a reply, Ben and his mother returned, and Jennifer flashed her a warning look, as if cautioning her not to say anything. Shelley had no desire to do so. The girl's resentment was not misplaced, and it only reinforced Shelley's own doubts about what she was doing. Perhaps she should take her life into her own hands and go back to London, she thought wearily. She couldn't go on running away forever and, strangely enough, being with Ben had helped her to get her emotions into perspective. She now knew she had never loved Mike, not even at the beginning, and if she clung to that knowledge, how could he hurt her?

'Dickon's suggested that you might like to stay at his house in Low Burton while I'm away,' Marsha announced, resuming her seat on the sofa as her son deposited the tea tray on the low table in front of her. 'You don't have any objections, do you, Jennifer? I know Shelley's entirely trustworthy.'

'Oh, really——' Shelley interrupted before the girl could say anything. 'I'll be perfectly all right here, Marsha. Good heavens, Mrs Carr lives in the house, and I'm not a nervous person!'

'Not usually, perhaps,' agreed Marsha, pouring tea into delicate porcelain cups. 'But, you forget, you've been ill, Shelley.' Her eyes met the younger woman's steadily. 'And I'd hate to think of you here alone if anything should happen.'

Shelley gasped. 'What could happen?' Her eyes turned helplessly to Ben's. 'I'm not an invalid!'

Ben shrugged, his expression controlled. 'What my mother is trying rather unsuccessfully to convey is the possibility that Berlitz might use the opportunity of her being away to come here——'

'To come here!' Shelley caught her breath. 'He wouldn't do that.'

'Wouldn't he?' Ben met her gaze guardedly. 'And if he did?'

'What is all this about?' Jennifer looked resentfully at each of them in turn. 'Who is this man you're talking about? And why should Shelley have cause to be afraid of him?'

'I'm not afraid of him,' responded Shelley quietly, and she found to her amazement that it was true. Somehow, by some means she was not prepared to examine too closely, the shadow of Mike's influence had ceased to intimidate her. Maybe it had something to with the feelings Ben had aroused inside her, or perhaps it was simply the fact that she had realised that there were things more important than being an associate producer.

Jennifer scowled. 'Then what——'

'It's my fault,' said Shelley quickly, silently appealing for Marsha's support. 'Mike Berlitz is my boss in London, and I'm afraid he wasn't very pleased when he discovered I'd had this—breakdown. He wants me back there, and Ben and his mother are concerned that he may use her absence to try and force me.'

Jennifer sniffed. 'Is that all!' She gave her fiancé an impatient look. 'I'm sure—Shelley—is quite capable of looking after her own interests. He's only a man, isn't he?'

'Only a man,' agreed Shelley, accepting the cup of tea Marsha handed to her. 'Really,' she added, avoiding Ben's eyes, 'I can handle it.'

'If you say so . . .'

Marsha shrugged, evidently prepared to give her the benefit of the doubt, but Shelley could feel Ben's frustration. But it was no good. If she stayed at the house in Ditchburn Lane, they both knew what would happen, and the more times they were together made it that much harder to contemplate their eventual break-up. As soon as Marsha's trip to London was over, Shelley was going to pick up the threads of her own life again, and if Ben had to be hurt, better now than later.

CHAPTER NINE

THERE was no opportunity for private conversation after that, and as if to assuage some of the frustration he was feeling, Ben became especially attentive to his fiancée. If it was a deliberate ploy on his part to make Shelley jealous, it succeeded, and the muscles of her face froze into a tight mask when he lounged on to the arm of Jennifer's chair and slipped a casual arm about her shoulders.

'Would you like me to run you down to the station on Tuesday morning?' he asked his mother, his hand lazily caressing the back of Jennifer's neck, and Shelley's nails drew blood in her palms.

'No. That won't be necessary, darling,' Marsha replied easily. 'I'll take the old Austin, unless Shelley will allow me to borrow her XR3.'

'Of course.' Shelley was glad of anything to distract her attention from Ben's lean brown fingers. 'I—borrow it with pleasure. I shan't be needing it.'

'No, you won't, will you? observed Ben harshly, abandoning his baiting and getting to his feet. 'Well—it's time we were leaving a Jennifer, are you ready?'

'When you are, darling,' she responded smugly, taking his hand to pull herself to her feet and retaining hold of it as they made their farewells. She gave Shelley a calculating smile. 'And if I don't see you again, Miss Hoyt——'

'What do you mean?' Marsha narrowly beat her son to the question. 'If you don't see Shelley again?'

'Oh——' Jennifer gave her future mother-in-law a disarming smile. 'Miss Hoyt—*Shelley*—was saying something about how quiet Craygill was when she compared it to London. I got the impression she was feeling homesick. Isn't that what you said, Shelley?'

It was what Jennifer had said, and they both knew it, but with three pairs of eyes watching her, short of calling her a liar, there was no way Shelley could avoid it. 'I think you misunderstood me, Jennifer,' she eventually replied, determined that Marsha should not be hurt by the girl's reckless words. 'If I compared Craygill to London, it could only have been in the most favourable of terms. I'd hardly be likely to feel homesick here, when I feel so at home already.'

Marsha's face, which only moments before had mirrored her dismay, cleared at once. 'Do you mean that, Shelley?' she exclaimed, her eyes wide and anxious. 'I thought for a moment you were going to tell me you were leaving.'

Shelley manufactured a smile from somewhere, and took the hand Marsha held out to her. 'No,' she said, reflecting that Jennifer had achieved the exact opposite to what she had intended. She squeezed Marsha's fingers. 'You're my family. The only family I've got.'

Ben and Jennifer departed a few moments later, and Shelley allowed Marsha to accompany them to the door alone. She was trying to come to terms with the fact that she had virtually committed herself to another six weeks at Craygill, and she wondered if Jennifer realised she was her own worst enemy.

'I'm sorry about that, my dear,' Marsha exclaimed, as she came back into the room. 'Jennifer can be so tactless at times.'

'It doesn't matter.'

'It does matter.' Marsha seated herself opposite and looked a little glum. 'Sometimes I wonder if she's right for Dickon after all.'

'Marsha!' Shelley swallowed quickly. 'Why do you say that?'

'Oh——' The older woman sighed. 'I sometimes feel as if I pushed him into it. But she seemed so sweet at first, and being a veterinary's daughter—it seemed the perfect match. Now I'm not so sure.'

Shelley moistened her lips. 'Surely—surely Dickon made his own decision.'

'Well, yes, he did, I know, but was it the right decision? I mean—what experience had he had?'

Shelley hesitated. 'I'm sure there were girls when he was at university.'

'I'm sure there were.' Marsha shrugged. 'But I never met any of them. They weren't—serious, if you know what I mean. The first girl he ever introduced me to was Jennifer, and that was mainly because she was Frank Chater's daughter.'

Shelley shook her head. She didn't want to hear this. 'Marsha, I'm sure you're exaggerating——'

'No, I'm not. You know what I'm like. You know how I've tried to push you and Charles together. It's crazy, isn't it? Particularly when my marriage was such a disaster. But that was mostly my fault, and you and Dickon are not as selfish as I was.'

'Oh, Marsha!' Shelley sucked in her breath. She would never have a better opportunity to be honest with her friend, and she knew it. 'Marsha, there's something I have to tell you.'

'What?' Marsha leant towards her. 'Don't tell me you really are getting bored at Craygill? I'll never hear the last of it if Jennifer's proved to be right.'

Shelley faltered. 'I—I——' She gripped the arms of her chair and sought desperately for the words. 'Marsha, did you know Dickon was attracted to me?'

'When he was younger? Of course.' Marsha was unperturbed by her confession, and Shelley realised she had said it badly. 'I told you he had a crush on you, didn't I? Heavens, that's not unusual. An impressionable boy and a successful woman! Oh, I see . . .' Shelley's anxious expression sent her off on another tack. 'You're suggesting that that may be why Dickon didn't get seriously involved with any girl at college. You could be right. Oh, I don't know what I'm worrying about. If he didn't want to marry Jennifer, he'd have said so.'

The moment had gone. Even without the sudden pealing of the telephone to signal its conclusion, the conversation was over, and Marsha went out of the room more cheerfully than she had come in.

She was back seconds later however. 'It's Charles,' she said, apparently indifferent to Shelley's agitation. 'Come on. He wants to speak to you.' Her eyes twinkled. 'He must have known we were talking about him.'

Charles was ringing to invite her to a Mozart recital being held in the town hall at Low Burton. It was a charity affair, in aid of funds for local hospitals, and although Shelley wanted to refuse, she really had no excuse. Besides, it was to be on Tuesday evening and, with Marsha away, she might be glad of the company, she admitted doubtfully. In any event, it would deter Ben from repeating his invitation, and maybe it would help to persuade him she meant what she said.

Marsha left early on Tuesday morning. She was driving to York to join the inter-city express for

King's Cross, and Shelley waved at the trim red XR3 until it disappeared from view.

But although Marsha's destination was familiar, Shelley felt no pangs of regret as she turned back into the house. She missed her apartment, of course, but that was mainly because of the things she kept in it. London, itself, held no such nostalgia, and she now understood Marsha's decision to make her home in the country.

The day passed slowly. In the morning, Shelley lazed in the garden, coming alert every time a vehicle passed on the lane below. But although two vans turned into the gates of Askrigg House, they were only tradesmen, and Mrs Carr dealt with them without troubling her guest.

To Shelley's relief, Mrs Carr herself served her lunch, and when she casually asked where Sarah was, she learned that the girl had called in sick the previous day. 'A tummy bug, or so her mother says, but I don't believe that,' declared the housekeeper staunchly. 'On Sunday afternoon, after Miss Manning's son and his fiancée had left, Miss Manning told her she wanted to have a word with her. Well, Sarah said it was her night off, and it was, so Miss Manning put it off until Monday morning.'

Shelley's tongue circled her upper lip. 'So—you think Sarah called in sick to avoid an interview with Miss Manning?'

Mrs Carr grimaced. 'Can you think of a better reason?'

Shelley shrugged. 'She could really be ill.'

'And pigs might fly,' said Mrs Carr scathingly. 'No. That young woman knows she's in trouble. You mark my words. I wouldn't put it past her to stay away from work for a week.'

Shelley sighed, resigning herself to the fact that

Marsha was unlikely to forgive this latest infringement. Sarah would have served herself better if she had reported for duty and made some attempt to defend her behaviour. By staying away from work, she was virtually admitting her guilt, and wasting Marsha's time into the bargain.

Charles called to take her to the recital at half-past-six. The performance was due to begin at seven o'clock, and as they took their seats he suggested that she might like to join him for supper afterwards.

'We should be out of here by half-past-nine,' he explained, admiring the flawless column of her throat revealed as she removed her jacket. 'I've asked my housekeeper to prepare a cold buffet. Premature perhaps, but with Marsha in London, I hoped you would forgive me.'

Shelley smiled a little tensely, all too well aware that Ben might be at the recital too, and remembering what had happened after her last outing with Charles. But she couldn't disappoint him, and adjusting the pointed collar of her dress with nervous fingers, she accepted his invitation.

She started to relax after the first half hour, and in the interval she accompanied Charles into the bar laid on for the occasion. He introduced her to a great many people, some of whom she remembered seeing at the operatic society's performance of *Camelot* some weeks ago, and Charles was evidently delighted to have her as his companion for the second time.

'I was beginning to think you'd never agree to come out with me again,' he declared, as they drove to his house afterwards. 'But Marsha suggested I should persevere, and she was right.'

Shelley sighed, wishing Marsha would mind her own business. The last thing she wanted was for

Charles to think there was any future in their relationship, and it didn't seem fair to accept his hospitality without making that clear.

'I think you ought to know, I have no intention of getting seriously involved with anyone,' she told him firmly, as they turned between the gates of a rambling Victorian mansion, situated on the outskirts of the small town. 'And if that means you'd like to take me straight home, then I'll quite understand. I just don't want you to get the wrong idea.'

Charles brought the car to a halt before the garage and then turned his head to look at her. His expression was shadowed in the light of the dash, but his tone was considering as he gave his response. 'That's a very sweeping statement,' he commented, his hands resting on the wheel. 'How do you know?' He paused. 'Unless there's someone else, of course.'

Shelley stiffened. 'Did Marsha tell you that, too?'

'Hardly.' Charles lifted his shoulders dismissingly. 'I shouldn't think she even suspects. But then, they do say the onlooker sees most of the game.'

Shelley's brows drew together. 'I beg your pardon?'

'Let's go inside and have some supper,' suggested Charles, turning off the ignition and opening his door. 'Mrs Sears will have gone to bed by now, and I'm sure you must be thirsty after all that Mozart. I know I am.'

Shelley had little choice but to accompany him, and for once she wished she had her own transport. Until Charles chose to drive her back to Craygill, she was forced to accept his hospitality, unless she called a cab, which would be rather ungracious.

The meal Charles's housekeeper had left for them was quite substantial. A pork pie, some quiche, cold meats and salad: Mrs Sears had obviously expected Shelley to be hungry. But although she accepted a slice of quiche and admired the decoration of a sherry trifle, Shelley did not feel comfortable, and only the wine proved a palliative to her confused nerves.

'You look troubled,' Charles said at last, when she refused his offer of a second glass of wine, and set the half-eaten slice of quiche back on the table. 'You needn't be. I don't intend to carry tales.'

Shelley stared at him blankly. 'Charles, I don't——'

'You and Ben,' he said briskly. 'I've seen the way you look at one another. Oh—I'm not saying it's gone any further than that, *yet*,' he added succinctly. 'But I imagine he's the reason you're so adamant about not getting involved.'

Shelley was stunned, and looked it. 'But how——' She shook her head. 'I mean, we never——'

'I should have suspected something that night I took you to see *Camelot*,' replied Charles drily. 'Ben wasn't exactly pleased to see us together, was he? And the evening when I came to dinner . . .' He studied the wine in his glass with a rueful expression. 'He could hardly take his eyes off you.'

'My God!'

Shelley gazed at him disbelievingly, and Charles sighed. 'I'm a doctor,' he said. 'I'm paid to diagnose people's problems. I suppose I've got so used to discriminating between what's real and what's imagined, I do it automatically. Sometimes I'm wrong. This time I don't think I am.'

Shelley expelled her breath weakly. 'But you haven't told Marsha.'

'No. Why would I? It's nothing to do with me.'

'But you've told me.'

'Yes.' Charles nodded. 'Because you're involved. And,' he lifted his shoulders, 'because I'm curious.'

'Curious?'

'Well,' he hesitated, 'I'm assuming from that blank statement you made in the car that you and he have no intention of—forgive the pun— consummating your relationship.'

'No.' Shelley could have lied and denied all knowledge of the matter, but she knew he wouldn't believe her. 'No, we haven't.'

'Might I ask why not?' Charles frowned. 'It surely can't be because of that silly child, Jennifer!'

'Jennifer's not a silly child,' retorted Shelley firmly. 'And—and partly, it's to do with her, of course.'

'But not all?'

'No.'

'You don't love him?'

'Please!' Shelley's face flamed. 'I don't think this has anything to do with you.'

'No, it doesn't.' Charles was unperturbed. 'But humour me—why should two people who evidently do care about one another choose not to do something about it?'

Shelley hesitated, and then, because it would be a relief to tell someone, she gave in. 'Ben doesn't love me,' she said heavily. 'He thinks he does, but he doesn't. It's one of those teenage fascinations he hasn't grown out of. I've known his mother for a lot of years, you see. When my parents were killed just after I left university, Marsha became my friend, and we've been friends ever since. Ben was just a boy, then. About fifteen, I suppose. I never thought of him in that way. It would have been ludicrous!'

Charles inclined his head. 'So when did you become aware that he wasn't a boy any longer? When you saw him again at Craygill?'

'Not exactly.' Shelley paused, and then added reluctantly: 'My car broke down on the way to Marsha's. Ben stopped and gave me a lift. I—didn't immediately recognise him.'

'But he recognised you.'

'Of course.' Shelley thrust impatient fingers into her hair, causing several strands to tumble confidingly beside her ears. 'I hadn't changed that much. He had.'

'I see.' Charles nodded. 'How intriguing!'

'It wasn't intriguing at all.' Shelley was indignant. 'It was embarrassing, actually.'

'Because you were attracted to him? Before you knew who he was, of course.'

Shelley sighed. 'You should have been a psychiatrist.'

'Why? Because I've made a perfectly reasonable deduction? Tell me, if Ben hadn't been Marsha's son, would you have felt differently?'

'Yes. No. I don't know.' Shelley was confused. 'You're missing the point. Ben isn't in love with me. He just *thinks* he is.'

'Because of this earlier attachment?'

'Yes.'

Charles looked thoughtful. 'Some might say that the length of the—so-called infatuation disproves your theory.'

'Well, it doesn't matter anyway,' retorted Shelley abruptly, getting to her feet. 'Will you take me home now?'

'Presently.' Charles was infuriatingly complacent. 'Tell me why it doesn't matter first.'

Shelley groaned. 'I should have thought the situation was blatantly obvious. I'm older than he is; I'm his mother's friend, not his; and can you imagine how Marsha would react if she—*suspected* our relationship was anything but platonic?'

'I see.' Charles nodded. 'So you're prepared to destroy the happiness of three people, just to satisfy some ridiculous sense of propriety.'

'Three people?'

'Well, you don't imagine Ben will make Jennifer happy, do you? If he doesn't love her.'

'You don't know he doesn't love her!' Shelley's fists clenched. 'You're basing your opinion on looks exchanged across a dinner table, and the unlikely humour of someone waiting outside a theatre in the pouring rain——'

'Not just on that,' Charles amended drily, coming to his feet. 'I saw you both in Low Burton on Saturday. Standing outside Hobsons, in the square. Are you going to deny he had his arm about you, or that either of you was aware of anything but yourselves?'

It was after eleven when Charles deposited Shelley back at Craygill. 'Thanks for the lecture,' she said, trying to make light of their conversation and failing abysmally. 'Seriously, though, you won't discuss this with Marsha, will you?'

'I'll treat it as a confidence,' he assured her, touching her cheek regretfully before she got out of the car. 'But don't ruin your life to please someone else, Shelley. You'll only regret it, and there's nothing like bitterness for destroying your youth.'

Mrs Carr had left a light burning in the hall, and after locking the door behind her, Shelley walked slowly into the living room. She was not tired. The conversation she had had with Charles had left her in a state of some agitation, and she thought perhaps a nightcap might help to calm her down.

A lamp provided a pool of light beside the chintz-covered sofa, and Shelley assumed Mrs Carr must have left it on, also for her benefit. What she was not prepared for was the man standing motionless in the shadows beside the window, and she started violently as he moved into the light.

'Ben!' she exclaimed, relief that it was no one else almost overwhelming her. 'Oh, God, you startled me! I thought for a minute you were Mike!'

'Would you have rather that it was he?' he enquired bleakly, the lamplight revealing hollows in his cheeks, which in day-light were not so evident. He shrugged his shoulders, taut beneath the casual elegance of a suede blouson. 'Did you have a pleasant evening?'

Shelley sighed. 'What are you doing here, Ben? Does Mrs Carr know? Or did you let yourself in with your key, after she'd retired for the night?'

'My mother's house is still my home, Shelley,' he retorted harshly. 'I don't have to have anyone's permission to come here. But, for the record, Mrs Carr let me in. It was she who told me where you were.'

Shelley moistened her lips. 'So why did you stay? You must have guessed I wouldn't be back until late.'

'Yes.' Ben inclined his head. 'You're right, of course. Except that I didn't come for the evening. I came for the night!'

Shelley caught her breath. 'You're crazy!'

'Why?'

'Well—because you can't—you can't stay here.'

'Why can't I?' Ben's mouth hardened. 'I do have a room of my own, you know.'

Shelley shook her head. 'This is madness!'

'Mrs Carr didn't seem to think so. Why shouldn't I spend the night in my mother's house?'

Shelley twisted her purse between her fingers. 'Your mother would not approve.'

'Why wouldn't she? She was all in favour of you staying with me.'

Shelley sighed. 'That was different. She wouldn't expect you to hang about here all evening, waiting for me to come back from—from the recital.'

Ben glanced briefly at his watch. 'Is that where you've been? I thought the recital was expected to be over by nine-thirty.'

Shelley bent her head. 'It finished about a quarter-to-ten. I went to Charles's house for supper afterwards.'

'Really?' Ben regarded her scathingly. 'I thought you said you didn't want to encourage him.'

'I don't.' Shelley shook her head. 'Oh—this is ridiculous! I don't have to answer to you, Ben. You're not my keeper.'

'No, I'm not, am I?' Ben thrust his hands deep into the pockets of his beige corded pants, and Shelley's heart ached for the lines of weariness etched upon his lean features. 'Okay.' He lifted his shoulders in a gesture of defeat. 'If that's the way you want it, who am I to argue?' He brushed past her, on his way to the door, and her arm tingled at the involuntary contact. 'But I will stay the night, if you don't object. I told Mrs Carr I would, and I'd hate to have to think of an explanation for changing my mind at midnight.'

Shelley stood in the living room long after the sound of his footsteps had faded. It was ironic, she thought, that Ben should feel resentful of Charles, when Charles himself was so sympathetic to the situation. She should have explained what they had been talking about, made it clear that Charles was their friend, not Ben's enemy. But to have done that would have opened up the whole question of their relationship again, and surely it was better to leave things as they were?

Extinguishing the downstairs lights, she finally went up to bed. Her brain was in a turmoil, and because she didn't expect to sleep, she spent some time in the bathroom, removing every scrap of make-up. Then, after putting on her nightgown, she slipped between the sheets, and tried to drum up some enthusiasm for the paperback novel she was reading.

But it was no good. The words were meaningless daubs on the paper, her mind bedevilled by thoughts of Ben, and the persistent suspicion that he was not sleeping either. And he needed his sleep, she thought anxiously. She could spend the next day in bed if she wanted, but he didn't have that privilege.

The sound of a door opening further along the corridor brought a quiver of anticipation, but although she heard footsteps on the landing, they did not stop at her door. As Mrs Carr's rooms were on the ground floor, it could only be Ben. Evidently, he was on his way downstairs, and she waited in some apprehension for him to come back up. Perhaps he had changed his mind, she thought, as the minutes stretched. Perhaps he had decided to go back to his own house, after all. She ought to hope he had, but she didn't, and she expelled her breath a little more freely, when she heard him coming back.

A door closed, and Shelley slumped against her pillows. Ridiculously, she had hoped he might see the light below her door and knock. But after the evening he had spent and the words they had exchanged, it had been a foolish aspiration. If she wanted to be with him, she would have to make the first move, and if she did she would be admitting that everything Charles had said was true.

With a feeling of desperation, she got out of bed and crossed the room to examine her reflection in the mirror of the dressing table. The image that met her startled gaze was not reassuring. She had thrust her fingers into her hair so many times, it stood out around her head in wild disorder. And her eyes were wary slits of green, the pale lids heavy with frustration. Even her cheeks were pallid, the kindness of the lamplight merely softening the lines that she found so offensive. Only her mouth looked vulnerable, she thought. For the rest, she looked every second of her age. Ben should see her now, he *should*. Perhaps then he would realise for himself what she had been trying to tell him.

Before second thoughts could weaken her resolve, Shelley swung about and strode out of her bedroom. Her long legs soon covered the dozen steps between her room and Ben's, and she had turned the handle and opened his door before realising the room was in darkness.

The sudden plunge into inky blackness was disorientating, and before she could recover herself, a lamp beside the bed was illuminated. Ben looked across at her from the tumbled disorder of his pillows, propped on one arm, the cream sheets falling away from the dark gold beauty of his body.

'Shelley!' he exclaimed, gazing at her with a mixture of anger and disbelief, and Shelley wished she had the strength to run. But, instead, she stood, letting his silver-lashed eyes move over her, assessing every inch of her scantily clad body.

'For Christ's sake!' he muttered at last, pushing back the covers and thrusting his feet out of bed, and as he came to his feet, she saw that he was naked. 'Are you crazy?' he added, the space between them narrowing to a handsbreadth. 'For God's sake, Shelley, you're shivering! What on earth have you been doing to yourself?'

Shelley found it incredibly difficult to say anything, but she had to stop him from touching her. If he took her in his arms now, she would not be able to resist, and that was not why she had come; not why she had come at all.

'Lo-look at me Ben!' she said unsteadily. 'Take a good look. Can you see these lines around my eyes? Have you noticed how sallow my skin is? And my hair! It's not soft and silky, it's thick— and coarse! And it's impossible to control. I'm thin. I'm not nicely rounded, I'm angular, but people think I'm attractive because I wear clothes well——'

'Will you stop that?' Ben's momentary astonishment quickly gave way to impatience, and ignoring her protests, his hands descended on her shoulders. 'For pity's sake, Shelley,' he groaned, resting his chin against her forehead and then, giving in to his emotions, he jerked her into his arms.

'You don't understand,' she breathed, her face pressed into the hollow of his throat. 'I'm not good for you. I came to tell you that. I came to show you what I'm really like. I'm not the sophisticated career woman you seem to think me. I'm a hysteric and a psychotic, and I've got a built-in propensity for disaster!'

'Oh, love!' Ben rubbed his cheek against hers.

'You have the craziest way of showing me you need me.'

'I—I don't need you,' she protested, even though her traitorous limbs were yielding to the muscled strength of his, and his laughter was low and intimate.

'You have the devil's own way of showing it,' he responded, his tongue wetting the hollow of her ear. 'Hell, Shelley, don't put me through any more misery! You have no idea what I went through while I was waiting for you this evening. God, I wanted to kill Brandeth! And when you came back and said you'd been to his house, I wanted to kill you, too.'

'Ben——'

'It's true.' He drew back to slide the straps of her nightgown off her shoulders, and when it pooled about her ankles, he picked her up in his arms and carried her to the bed. 'I love you,' he told her huskily, lowering himself beside her, and as his lips explored the sensitive skin on the inner curve of her arm, the soft mass of hair that furred his thighs caressed her stomach. 'And to me you'll always be beautiful,' he added, his lips slanting hungrily across hers, so that any further objections Shelley might have made were stifled by the searching pressure of his mouth . . .

CHAPTER TEN

SHELLEY was jolted into consciousness by the instinctive awareness that something had wakened her. For a few moments the unaccustomed warmth of Ben's body curled at her back, his arm looped possessively across her hip, caused a delicious feeling of lethargy to encompass her, but then the realisation that it was already light outside proved a potent deterrent to what she was thinking

Grasping the wrist of the arm that was curled beneath her head, Shelley examined the face of his watch. It was half-past-seven, and her heart leapt into her throat. What had probably disturbed her was Mrs Carr, collecting the morning's milk from the doorstep, and any time now the housekeeper could appear, with a tray of early morning tea for her employer's son.

'Ben!' Turning hastily on to her back, Shelley dislodged his arm, and his hand shifted to lie confidingly between her thighs. It was a devastating distraction, and one to which she was not immune, and she lifted the errant member and returned it to him.

'Will you stop moving about,' he mumbled presently, burying his face more deeply into the tangled curtain of her hair. His hand sought the rounded swell of her breasts with evident satisfaction. 'Mmm, I thought I had only dreamed it.' His eyes flickered lazily. 'But I didn't, did I?'

Once before, Shelley had thought she might drown in his eyes, and now, with their dark brilliance muted to a smouldering charcoal, she

was briefly convinced there could be no kinder
fate.

'It's late,' she breathed, without much conviction, and Ben shifted so that she could feel the
stirring length of him against her.

'It's early,' he contradicted her huskily, after
giving his watch a careless glance. 'I don't have to
be at the surgery until nine.'

'But, Mrs Carr——'

'To hell with Mrs Carr,' he retorted thickly, and
his mouth crushed hers just as the bedroom door,
which hadn't been properly closed the night
before, was thrust open.

Shelley closed her eyes in dismay. What she had
feared had happened, she thought weakly. Mrs
Carr would now know why Ben had driven all the
way out to Craygill when his mother wasn't even
at home, and she was bound to tell Marsha, unless
Ben could persuade her otherwise.

It took Ben's harsh ejaculation and a shudder-
ing moan from someone else to convince Shelley
that something worse had happened. Opening her
eyes, she saw Ben staring over her head at the
door, his face twisted into a mask of weary
frustration. Then she, too, turned her head, just in
time to see Marsha herself disappearing into the
corridor.

Ten minutes later, Shelley entered the morning
room and found Ben's mother hunched at the
table, a cup of coffee clutched between her palms.
The remnants of an early breakfast littered the
crisp white tablecloth—a rack of toast, marmalade,
a pot of butter—but it was evident from Marsha's
attitude that food no longer interested her. She
was dressed in the same clothes in which she had
left home the day before, Shelley saw in surprise,

and briefly she wondered why Marsha had not stayed over, as she had planned to do. Unless someone had warned her about the relationship between her son and her friend, Shelley speculated uneasily. She couldn't help the unworthy suspicion that there might be some connection between Marsha's unexpected return and Sarah's convenient absence.

Ben had been less willing to draw conclusions. On the contrary, once the first shock of his mother's appearance had worn off, he had been quite philosophic.

'It was bound to happen sooner or later,' he argued gently, preventing Shelley from leaping out of bed and following her. 'I'm sorry she had to find out in such a brutal way, but there's nothing we can do about it now.'

'I have to see her. I have to speak to her,' Shelley had retorted fiercely, fighting the insidious temptation to stay where she was. 'Ben, let me go! *Please!* I have to try and explain. Though goodness knows how I'm going to do it!'

He had let her go eventually, but not before he had elicited a promise from her not to speak to his mother until he was with her. 'We can do this together, or not at all,' he told her roughly, brushing her bruised lips with the pad of his thumb. 'Get dressed. I'll meet you in fifteen minutes. And stop looking so anxious. It's not the end of the world.'

But it seemed like it. The end of her world, at least, Shelley reflected bitterly, as she stood just inside the door of the morning room. She had ignored Ben's advice and thrown on her clothes after the most cursory rinses of her face, and with her hair screwed into a hasty knot, she felt exactly like a schoolgirl up before the headmistress. But she had to talk to Marsha before Ben appeared. She had to try and tell her that she had no intention of taking him away from his fiancée, or of doing anything which might cause Marsha any pain.

'Marsha,' she ventured now, her voice soft and breathy, and although the older woman did not look up, the sudden stiffening of her shoulders was revealing. 'Marsha, it's not like you think.'

Marsha replaced her coffee cup in its saucer with excessive care. Then, hooking the heel of one hand beneath her chin, she lifted her head. 'No?'

'No.' Shelley moistened her dry lips, appalled by the bluish tinge of Marsha's features. The older woman looked more than tired, she looked bone weary, and Shelley knew she would never forgive herself for what she had done. 'Marsha, you have to believe me!'

'Believe what?' Marsha waved a bitter hand in the air. 'That you were not in my son's bed? That you hadn't just spent the night with him? That you were not making love with him?'

Shelley sighed. 'I know how it looks, but——'

'Oh, Shelley!' Before she could say any more, Marsha's impassioned voice prevented her. 'How could you? How could you? And to think—I trusted you!'

'Marsha, listen to me——'

'Why should I listen to you?' Marsha's lips twisted convulsively. 'My God! And I felt sorry for you! When you came here in such distress, stringing that tale about Mike Berlitz, I really wanted to help you. I didn't know you were using me to get at my son!'

'I wasn't!' Shelley's voice broke. 'It wasn't like that. For pity's sake, Marsha, what do you take me for?'

'I don't know, do I?' Marsha retorted coldly. 'I thought I did, but I don't. For all I know, you may have led Berlitz on like he says; *used* him! A woman who would seduce her best friend's son—a boy of twenty-five——'

'I'm not a *boy*.' Ben's calm impassive voice was like a draught of cool water in the desert, and Shelley turned to him tremulously, her eyes wide with pain and humiliation. 'What have you been saying to her, Mother? She didn't seduce me, if that's what you're accusing her of.'

'Keep out of this, Dickon.' Marsha pushed back her chair and got to her feet, supporting herself on the rim of the table. 'This is between Shelley and me. I'll speak to you later.'

'You'll speak to me now,' retorted Ben grimly. 'I'm not a child, Mother. You can't accuse Shelley without accusing me. For Christ's sake, *I* seduced *her*! Is that blatant enough for you?'

'Ben, please——' Shelley spread an arm as if to stop him. 'You didn't seduce me. Both of us know that. And you're only making things worse by getting involved.'

'Getting involved!' echoed Ben incredulously. 'I'm not *getting* involved, I am involved. Shelley, let me tell my mother how it is. The sooner she understands the facts, the better.'

'*No*——' began Shelley faintly, but Marsha's strangled: 'What facts?' overrode her.

'I'm in love with Shelley, Mother,' Ben declared firmly, in spite of the younger woman's moan of protest. 'This isn't an affair. I want to marry her. And we can do that with or without your blessing; it's up to you.'

'Marry her!'

Marsha almost choked on the words, and Shelley gave Ben a look of mortification. 'It's not

true!' she exclaimed, ignoring his warning impreca-
tion. 'I have no intention of marrying Ben—
Dickon! It's like you say—he is still a boy; an
idealist. What we've done is wrong, but not
irretrievable. If you'd just stop hating me long
enough to listen to me, I'm sure you'd understand.'

The slamming of a door behind them was the
first indication Shelley had that Ben had walked
out. Seconds later the outer door slammed, too,
and in spite of her conviction, a knife-like spasm
twisted in her stomach.

'I think you'd better go, too, Shelley,' said
Marsha at last, sinking wearily back into her chair.
'Whatever you say, I'll never forgive you for
causing this rift between Dickon and me. Maybe it
was like you said. Maybe Dickon was equally to
blame. But you're older, Shelley. You should have
stopped it before it began. Or was it simply a way
to get Mike Berlitz out of your mind?'

Shelley shook her head. 'You don't believe that.'

'I don't know what to believe.' Marsha spread
her hands. 'It's obvious Berlitz still wants you, but
how can I be sure?'

Shelley's shoulders sagged. 'You saw Mike then.'

'Yesterday, yes.' Marsha's expression darkened.
'For precisely fifteen minutes. Then I walked out.'

Shelley gazed at her blankly. 'You walked out?'

'His—terms—were not acceptable then,' stated
Marsha flatly. 'Now, I'm not so sure.'

Shelley blinked. 'What do you mean?'

'It was a ruse,' said Marsha, tracing the rim of
her coffee cup with her finger nail. 'As you
suspected, didn't you?' Her eyes met Shelley's
bitterly. 'I should have known. Capitol Television
has never been known for promoting provincial
artists.'

'You're not a provincial artist, Marsha,' protested Shelley fiercely. 'What did he say? I thought it was Tim Hedley you were going to see.'

'It was. He was there.' Marsha shrugged. 'Unfortunately, as you should know, he takes his orders from Mike Berlitz. And Berlitz had other things in mind.'

Shelley shook her head. 'I'm sorry.'

'So am I.' Marsha grimaced. 'If I'd known my promotion was contingent upon persuading you to change your mind, I'd never have left Craygill. I wish to God I hadn't.'

'Oh, Marsha!'

Shelley would have gone to her then, but the older woman's outstretched arm prevented her. 'No,' she said. 'I don't need your sympathy, Shelley. Like I said, I wish you would go. I'm sorry, but you're no longer welcome at Askrig House.'

The Capitol Television building stood in Prince Albert Road, close to Regent's Park. In her early days with the company, Shelley used to bring sandwiches to work and eat her lunch in the park, throwing crusts to the pigeons that flocked around the visitors. Even in winter there were always plenty of takers for the crumbs of bread and cake that found their way onto the footpaths, and now, in high summer, the throngs of children guaranteed good pickings for the hungry birds.

Today, however, Shelley was in no mood to pay attention to the crowds making their way into the park. Leaving her car in the over-crowded lot that adjoined the complex, she walked swiftly into the television building. She had an early morning appointment with her employer, and she had the feeling that no matter how confident she felt, this was not going to be a pleasant interview.

'Why, hello, Miss Hoyt,' exclaimed George Tomlin, the commissionaire, as she crossed the lobby. 'Long time, no see. You been on holiday or something?'

'Or something,' said Shelley drily, as the lift doors opened to her summons. 'How are you, George? And how's Mrs Tomlin?'

'Better in health than temper,' the old commissionaire declared, as he always did. 'You take care now, you're looking rather peaky.'

'Too many late nights,' Shelley assured him, as the lift doors closed behind her. It was the kind of comment he expected, and she had no intention of getting involved in any personal discussion of her health.

She travelled up alone to the fourteenth floor, taking the opportunity to check that no errant strands of hair were escaping from the pins that secured it at her nape. The wall of smoky glass that faced the doors gave back her reflection in shadowy detail, and she was satisfied with the severity of the black pencil-slim skirt and matching jacket. Only her face stood out in sharp relief, the pallor George Tomlin had noted accentuating the brilliance of her hair.

The suite of rooms Mike Berlitz used occupied most of the penthouse floor. As well as office accommodation, he had a fully equipped service flat, that for a time Shelley had been as familiar with as her own, and a large lounge for entertaining, when members of the governing body gathered for their monthly meetings.

Diane Sanderson, Mike's secretary-cum-personal assistant, was already at her desk when Shelley walked into the suite of offices, and her eyes narrowed speculatively as she took in the other girl's sombre appearance.

'Is Mike expecting you?' she asked, lying back in her chair and regarding Shelley over the arch of her fingers. 'He didn't say anything to me. I thought you were in the Lake District or somewhere.'

'Was,' said Shelley politely. 'And it was Wensleydale. And yes, he is expecting me. Shall I go straight in?'

'Be my guest.' Diane sounded as if she couldn't care less, but as Shelley crossed the thickly carpeted floor to the heavy wooden doors leading to the inner sanctum, she speedily abandoned her indifference. 'Miss Hoyt is on her way in, Mr Berlitz,' she informed him, pressing down the intercom, and Shelley's smile was faintly amused as she propelled the heavy doors inward.

It was a theatrical entrance, but she couldn't help it. She had always thought Mike had had the doors installed deliberately so that anyone entering his office would be immediately intimidated. She supposed they had once intimidated her. But not now. This morning she simply used them as a means to an end, and the man who came to meet her, across a vast expanse of burgundy broadloom, was immediately aware of her cool detachment.

Mike Berlitz was forty-five, but looked younger. He was a slimly built man of medium height, who had not allowed his sedentary occupation to ruin either his health or his appearance. He played squash regularly, and spent the occasional week at a health spa, and in consequence he could still wear the same size in suits as he had worn when he was a youth. He was a good-looking man, whose sandy-brown hair had not yet begun to thin, and in his position as chief executive he was quite a heart-throb among the girls on his staff.

There was no trace of animosity in his face now

as he met Shelley in the middle of the floor, and had she not had that telephone conversation with him, she would never have suspected his true feelings. 'My dear,' he exclaimed, taking a resisting hand between both of his and holding it tightly. 'I'm delighted you've decided to cut short your— convalescence. Livingstone's been an adequate substitute, of course, but he doesn't have your flair or potential.'

Shelley withdrew her hand and stood back from him. 'It's very kind of you to say so, Mike,' she thanked him politely. 'Do I take it the job's still mine? In spite of everything?'

Briefly, a look of confusion crossed his face, but it was quickly concealed. 'Of course, the job's still yours,' he responded, though his eyes were guarded. 'You know how much I've missed you. I haven't exactly kept it a secret.'

Shelley moistened her lips. 'That isn't what I meant, Mike, and you know it.' She took a deep breath. 'I would like to hear what you have to say about Marsha Manning. I'm wondering what excuse you'll give for causing her so much unnecessary heartache.'

Mike's eyes narrowed, but after a moment he glanced behind him. 'I suggest we sit down and discuss this over a cup of coffee,' he said pleasantly. 'You've obviously been given some false information, and I'd welcome the opportunity to set the record straight.'

'No.' Ignoring his invitation, Shelley stood her ground. 'Just tell me whose idea it was to put the suggestion to Marsha. And who dared to try and manipulate me through her!'

Mike stiffened. '*Dared*, Shelley? That's a rather emotive word.'

'It's rather an emotive situation,' she retorted

tensely. 'Someone deliberately allowed Marsha to think you were serious about the importance of her work, and then calmly told her it was all a lie!'

'It wasn't a lie.' Mike's jaw was working. 'It was an offer, made in good faith——'

'Subsequent upon my doing as I'm told!'

'Grow up, Shelley!' Mike's control snapped and he gazed at her angrily. 'We all know you're coming back sooner or later. You don't have a choice. And why shouldn't I try and precipitate the situation with a little sweetener of my own!'

'A sweetener!' Shelley caught her breath. 'You don't have any conception what you've done, do you?'

'I've made a perfectly acceptable offer,' retorted Mike harshly. 'For Christ's sake, I could have used other methods to force your hand. You should be thanking me for giving Manning half a chance!'

'Half a chance!' Shelley gasped. 'Marsha doesn't need your patronage! Her work is recognised all over the world. It's you who should be begging her to let you screen her life!'

'I don't notice any other television station beating a path to her door,' retorted Mike nastily. 'And in any case, she's not the real point at issue, is she? *You* are.'

Shelley shook her head. 'I never realised you could be so vindictive——'

'That's because you don't live in the real world, Shelley. You've been cushioned for so long——'

'Cushioned?'

'Yes, cushioned!' Mike made an impatient gesture. 'How far do you think *you'd* have got if I hadn't taken you in hand? Okay—so you had a flair for current affairs reporting. But that's not unique.'

'Thank you.'

Shelley weathered the blast of his contempt without flinching, even though inside she was sick to her stomach. Was it true then? Had she only become successful because Mike had made her that way? Were all the sly innuendos, thrown at her over the years, the true extent of her ability? She didn't want to believe it, but what else could she do?

'Oh, Shelley——' As if sensing the turmoil being fought behind her frozen features, Mike halted his tirade. 'This isn't the way I wanted things to be. We belong together; in work and out of it. Let's stop this bickering and get down to what really matters: when will you be coming back?'

Shelley's nails dug into the leather of her handbag. 'I suppose that depends on what you mean by "coming back",' she responded, holding up her head. 'You know my feelings about our personal relationship. If you mean—when can I return to my position as associate producer, I'd probably only need a few days.'

Mike expelled his breath heavily. 'Shelley——'

'Yes?'

'Shelley, you know that isn't good enough.'

'No?' She deliberately misunderstood him. 'I should have thought a few days was quite reasonable——'

'That's not what I mean, and you know it.' He took a step towards her, but once again she eluded him. 'Shelley, when are you going to stop all this fooling about? You know what I want, and I won't settle for less. What do I have to do to convince you, that I won't take no for an answer?'

Shelley sighed. So, she thought wearily, ultimately it did come down to this: either she toed the line in their personal relationship, or Mike made things difficult for her in other ways.

'And if I refuse?' she countered, realising how unimportant his reply had become.

'You won't.' Mike was confident. 'We've been through too much together.'

'We haven't been through anything!' Shelley gazed at him incredulously. 'You *used* me—and maybe I used you, too, only I didn't know it at the time. But at least I can console myself with the fact that as soon as I realised what you were doing, I put an end to it.'

'You didn't put an end to it,' he contradicted her harshly. 'You may have interrupted things for a while, but our feelings for one another never changed.'

Shelley shook her head. 'I don't have any feelings for you, Mike,' she told him steadily, only now aware of how tenuous their relationship had been. 'I liked you once. I was even attracted to you, in a hero-worshipping sort of way, but that didn't last. I did grow up, Mike. The trouble is, you haven't.'

The eloquence with which she delivered her statement evidently surprised him, and it was several seconds before he formulated a reply. 'I think you should consider your position very carefully before making any rash statements,' he declared at last. The smile he forced was scarcely more than a splitting of his tightly clenched lips. 'I don't think you quite understand the position. You need me, Shelley. I do not need you.'

She had known where their argument was heading, but even so she had to clarify her position. 'You're saying that my employment with Capitol Television is subject to certain—conditions?'

Mike's nostrils flared. 'Something like that.'

'The same conditions you put to Marsha, one

supposes,' murmured Shelley quietly, and as if realising his ultimatum was not going the right way, Mike overcame her protests and grasped her by the shoulders.

'Why are you doing this, Shelley?' he demanded, thrusting his face close to hers, and she turned her head aside to avoid his angry expression. 'For heaven's sake, you can't intend to turn down all that I can give you! Take whatever time you need, but come back as my wife!'

'No, Mike!' With a supreme effort Shelley broke free of him, and as she did so there was a knock at the door of his office.

'Blast!'

With an oath, Mike was forced to let her escape him, and Shelley quickly opened the door to facilitate her departure.

'I'm sorry to interrupt you, Mr Berlitz,' began Diane, in carefully controlled tones, but Shelley was aware of the other girl's shock and amazement as she strode towards the door.

'*Shelley!*'

Mike's angry command brought an enquiring pause, and she arched one dark brown eye-brow. 'Yes?'

'If you—if you walk out of here, you won't come back,' he threatened, casting Diane a warning glance, but Shelley only shrugged.

'I never expected anything else,' she told him, stepping into the corridor, and although she knew she might regret it later, right then she felt a marvellous sense of relief.

CHAPTER ELEVEN

SHELLEY poured herself a cup of coffee and carried it into the living room of the flat. Then, kicking off her shoes, she sank down upon the chesterfield, examining the letter again as she sipped the steaming liquid. She had been offered the job, she told herself fiercely, wishing she could summon more enthusiasm for the fact. John Sadler had not allowed the indifferent reference Mike Berlitz had given her to influence his decision. He liked her ideas. He had told her so. And against all the odds, she was being given a chance to survive on her own merits.

So why wasn't she excited about it? Why wasn't she calling her friends, and arranging a party; anything to celebrate the victory of proving her independence?

She sighed, and putting the coffee cup aside, she rested her head back against the buttoned leather upholstery. She knew the answer, of course, had acknowledged it through a dozen nights of hollowed-eyed sleeplessness. Even the five or six weeks that had elapsed since she left Craygill had barely blunted the sharpness of her anguish, and she was gradually coming to realise that some things never changed.

She was in love with Ben Seton. Like Charles had said, she had been attracted to him long before she realised who he was, and from then on she had been fighting a losing battle. It didn't alter the situation. He was still Marsha's son, and because of her selfishness she had lost the

172

friendship of someone she cared for dearly. But she also knew that given the same circumstances, she would probably do it all again.

She was not proud of that admission, though there were times when she tended towards the view that anyone who was prepared to put themselves through purgatory, should have had some compensation for doing so. Nevertheless, the future was bleak indeed without even Marsha's friendship, and Shelley missed her letters and the 'phone calls they had shared.

She couldn't help wondering what had happened after her ignominious departure. She had even hoped that Ben might write and tell her he understood. Surely, by now, he must have realised that she was right? In this, at least, his mother would share Shelley's conviction.

But the days had stretched into weeks—almost six weeks now—and Shelley had given up hope of ever hearing from either of them again. It must be only a matter of weeks before Ben and Jennifer were getting married. With the arrangements for the wedding, Marsha would have no time to worry about her. And afterwards ... Shelley shook her head. Did she really want to know that Ben was someone else's husband?

Pushing these thoughts aside, Shelley picked up her empty cup and carried it into the kitchen. She had to stop thinking about the past and concentrate on the future. She had a real chance now. With the offer of a job with National Television she could compete on her own terms, without the suspicion that someone else was secretly pulling the strings.

The intercom which connected her flat with the front entrance buzzed as Shelley was examining the fridge, wondering what she should have for dinner. She wasn't hungry. She seldom was these days, and the pre-cooked meals she provided herself with were often consigned to the waste disposal.

Now, glad to be diverted from a task she seldom welcomed, Shelley crossed the living room to lift the receiver, wondering belatedly who it might be. In the early days following her return to London, the days after that stormy interview at Capitol Television, Mike had made several visits to the flat, but all to no avail. He had even accosted her once, on her way to do some shopping, and virtually threatened her with dire consequences should she continue to ignore his offer, but Shelley had been adamant. Even though she was out of a job, and in Mike's opinion likely to stay that way, she had not been alarmed by his intimidation. And if she was obliged to take a less-demanding post, she would keep her independence. That—and the remnants of her self respect—were all she really had left.

Now, however, it did cross her mind to wonder whether Mike had heard of her successful interview at National Television and had come to make a counter offer. She hoped not. She had begun to believe she was free of his machinations, and it troubled her to think he might still be marking time.

'Yes?' Her voice was a little terse in consequence as she spoke into the receiver, and her caller sounded faintly apologetic as she identified herself.

'Shelley? It's Marsha. Can I come up?'

To say that Shelley was shocked was to put too fine a point upon it. She was stupefied; *stunned*; rendered almost speechless by the sound of that so-familiar voice. Without thinking, without even trying to speculate why she might have come,

Shelley said: 'Yes. Come up,' in a strangled voice, and then pressed the release catch almost automatically as she slumped beside the door.

She had scarcely gathered her wits when the tap came at the door. Having enabled the other woman to open the outer door, Marsha had been able to mount the two flights of stairs to Shelley's floor, and her tentative summons caused no minor panic in Shelley's chest. What did Marsha want? she asked herself anxiously. What awful calamity had brought her all the way to London? Surely, if something had happened to Ben, Marsha would have written. It wasn't like her to make the journey unannounced.

Realising she could not put off the moment indefinitely, Shelley took a deep breath and opened the door. 'Marsha,' she said huskily, but she could hear the edge of hysteria in her voice. 'Wh—what a surprise! You—you should have let me know you were coming.'

Marsha said nothing for a moment, her keen, painter's eye observing more than Shelley would have wished. In the space of a few seconds she noted the starkly drawn features, the nervously fluttering hands, the revealing air of finely stretched muscle, that warned of a brittle fragility, not even acknowledged by Shelley herself.

Then, because of what she could see, and because of what she had learned, she held out her arms, and Shelley collapsed into them. With an eagerness long denied both women embraced, and only when her tears threatened to soak Marsha's tweed-clad shoulder did Shelley manage to pull herself together.

'Oh, God, I'm sorry,' she said, sniffing, and stepping back into the apartment. 'Come in, please! You don't know how glad I am to see you.'

'I have a fairly good idea,' remarked Marsha drily, smothering what sounded suspiciously like a sniff herself. 'Put the kettle on, there's a good girl. I think we could both do with a good strong cup of tea.'

With the kettle plugged in, and her mother's best porcelain cups decorating the tea tray, Shelley turned to find Marsha propped against the frame of the kitchen door. 'How domesticated!' she murmured lightly, though her expression was far from frivolous. 'No. I don't want anything to eat, thank you. I had a quite satisfactory lunch, and I'm planning on having an even more satisfactory dinner.'

'Oh.' Shelley forced a smile. 'You're staying in town then?'

'Temporarily,' agreed Marsha, affecting an interest in the pattern of the rubber floor tiles. 'As a matter of fact, I'm here to discuss the format of a television profile with Tim Hedley. Apparently your friend Mr Berlitz had second thoughts about its viability.'

'Oh, Marsha!' Shelley was genuinely delighted for her friend. 'When did this come about?'

'A few days ago.' Marsha was offhand. 'It couldn't have come at a better time. I was looking for a reason to come to London.'

'You were?' The kettle boiled and Shelley could hide her confusion in filling the teapot. 'Why?'

'Because I wanted to see you.' Marsha was honest. 'Mike Berlitz isn't the only one who's had second thoughts.' She paused, and then continued uncomfortably: 'I don't expect you to believe this, Shelley, but I wish I hadn't jumped to such predictable conclusions.'

'Oh—well——' Shelley picked up the tray, and because it was expected of her, Marsha moved back into the living room. There was an awkward little silence while Shelley set the tray on a glass-topped coffee table beside the couch and then, equally because she felt it was expected of her, Shelley added: 'Couldn't we just—forget about it?'

Marsha seated herself on the chesterfield before replying, but when she did, Shelley's cheeks flamed with colour. 'I don't think we can—forget about it,' she demurred. 'For whatever reason, my son is in love with you, Shelley. I've had to accept it, and I think you must, too.'

Shelley made no attempt to deal with the cups and saucers. Her hands were shaking so much, she was sure she would either spill the tea or drop the cups or both. Instead, she lowered her trembling body on to the arm of the chair opposite, and gazed at the other woman with something akin to distraction.

'It's true,' said Marsha, taking over the role of hostess, and pouring the tea with rather more self-possession. 'And I'm hoping that Charles was not mistaken when he told me that you cared for him, too. Not Charles, of course.' A fleeting smile briefly lit her features. 'And to think I thought the bad experience you had had with Mike Berlitz was responsible for your indifference to him!'

Shelley shook her head. 'Marsha——'

'Not yet, my dear. Let me finish.' Marsha added milk and, ignoring Shelley's protest, several spoonfuls of sugar, to one of the dainty cups and held it out to her. 'Go on,' she said. 'Drink it. The sugar will sustain you, and you look as though you need it.'

Shelley took the cup in both hands and obediently raised it to her lips. It was unbearably sweet, but mindful of Marsha's warning gaze, she drank it down steadily, finally finding some strength of her own in the dark brown strength of the liquid.

'Good.' Marsha took the empty tea cup from her and replaced it on the tray. 'It's obvious you've not been looking after yourself as you should. Which seems to prove Charles's supposition that he's more perceptive than I am.'

'Charles?' Shelley tried to think coherently. 'What has he been saying?'

'Not a lot.' Marsha lifted her shoulders. 'He only succeeded in convincing me that I had to do something about—well, about both of you.'

'Both of us?' echoed Shelley anxiously. 'You mean me—and Ben?' She stiffened. 'Is Ben all right? You didn't say.'

Marsha hesitated. 'He's not ill, if that's what you mean,' she murmured diffidently. 'But—oh, Shelley! you will agree to see him, won't you? I know he won't ask you himself—not after what you said. But if you do care for him at all, then please do this for me. I know my behaviour hasn't always been admirable, but I love my son, Shelley.' She shook her head. 'I love you both.'

Shelley stared at her blankly. 'I don't understand . . .'

'It's quite simple.' Marsha cleared her throat. 'A week after you left Craygill, Dickon broke off his engagement.'

Shelley gulped. 'He broke it off?'

'Yes.' Marsha sighed. 'Oh—it wasn't quite without its drama. Dickon and I were hardly speaking, you see, and he'd told me in no uncertain terms that as soon as he decently could, he was leaving. Of course, with Frank Chater's health still causing some concern, he felt obliged to stay on, for the present at least, and I suppose I still hoped he might change his mind.' She grimaced. 'I was wrong.'

Shelley frowned. 'But if Mr Chater——'

'It was Sarah,' said Marsha, interrupting her. 'You remember Sarah, don't you? Well, I fired her, and to get back at me, she carried some tale to Jennifer about you and Dickon.' She gave a weary shrug. 'There was the most God-awful row!'

'Oh, no!'

'Oh, yes.' Marsha shook her head. 'It was exactly the opportunity Dickon had been waiting for.'

Shelley gazed uncertainly at her. 'He left?'

'No.' Marsha made a negative gesture. 'Thank God, not yet at any rate. But he has applied for a job in West Africa, and if he gets it . . .' Her voice tailed away, but her meaning was evident.

Shelley moistened her lips, 'And—and you want me to persuade him not to go?'

'Yes. No. At least—oh, Shelley, I know I'm doing this badly, but I'm not here purely for selfish reasons. I would have written, but I was afraid you wouldn't read my letter, and it wasn't easy, finding an excuse to come to London.'

'But why did you need an excuse?' exclaimed Shelley helplessly. 'Surely you knew I would never turn you away.'

'Oh, my dear——' Marsha bent her head in some embarrassment. 'After the way I treated you, you have every right to hate me. I let you think you could depend upon me, and then I let you down so badly.'

'No.' Shelley left her perch and went to sit on the chesterfield beside her friend. 'No, you didn't let me down, Marsha, I let you.' She made a sound of self-derision. 'I didn't want to hurt you. I was sure it was just—just infatuation. On Ben's part, at least. I'm older than he is. I thought I had more sense. I knew I was deceiving you, but I thought that was better than ruining Ben's life!'

'By admitting you were in love with him, you

mean?' suggested Marsha quietly, and Shelley hesitated only a moment before nodding. 'So you will go and see him then?'

Shelley expelled her breath on a gulp. 'I—I don't know if I should.'

'You must!' Marsha was determined. 'I haven't told you everything. Dickon—*Ben*—hasn't been well——'

'But you said——'

'I said he wasn't ill now, and he's not.' Marsha caught Shelley's fluttering hands and held on to them. 'Listen to me, Shelley. He got soaked one night, helping Dave Sanderson's prize heifer to calve. The stupid animal got out of the barn, and she was bogged down in the mud flats by the river when they ran her to ground. It was a filthy night, and Dickon caught a chill. If I'd known anything about it, I'd have insisted he let me fetch him to Craygill, and I'd have taken care of him; but I didn't. It was Charles who told me what was going on. Dickon's daily woman called him when she found him half-unconscious on the kitchen floor.'

Shelley's stomach heaved. 'Oh, God!'

Marsha nodded. 'You can imagine how I felt. It was pneumonia, of course, and for a couple of days, he hardly knew who I was. Anyway, by the time he had recovered, he and I had achieved at least a measure of civility, and although we don't mention you, we're not so distant with one another as we were.'

'Oh, Marsha!'

'Which brings me to the same question: will you go and see him? He's living on his nerves—just as you are—and Charles insists that I'm to blame for not realising what was going on.'

Shelley swallowed. 'Go to Craygill, you mean?'

'No.' Marsha shook her head, and Shelley looked confused. 'The Metropolitan Hotel,' her friend explained gently. 'As Charles insisted he took a couple of weeks holiday, I persuaded him to come to London with me.'

Shelley drew back. 'Does he know you're here?'

'No.' Marsha sighed. 'I doubt if he would have let me come, if he had known what I intended. He's very proud, Shelley, and I think you've convinced him you really don't care.'

The Metropolitan Hotel stood in Piccadilly, its elegant façade looking with some disdain on the less imposing edifices surrounding it. Once falling into disrepair, it had now been modernised by an Arab consortium, and Shelley was reluctantly impressed as she crossed its cushioned floor.

Marsha had told her that the rooms she and Ben had taken were on the fourth floor and, ignoring the enquiring gaze of a porter, Shelley made directly for the lifts.

'Four,' she said, in answer to the lift attendant's obsequious request, and endeavoured to give her attention to her surroundings as the mirrored cage swept upwards.

There was a padded bench in the lift, a remnant of the days when hotels like these were the exclusive haunt of the rich and famous, who regarded standing as something of an imposition. But Shelley was too tense to appreciate the luxury, and when the gate was opened at the fourth floor, she quickly hurried out.

Room 425 was at the farthest end of a carpeted corridor, and as she hastened along it, it occurred to her that Ben could be out. Just because Marsha expected him to be getting ready for dinner at this

time was no reason to be assured of the fact and,
as it was almost half-past six, he could be
downstairs in the bar.

Her fingers shook as she raised them to knock,
and she cast an anxious glance at her appearance.
She should have worn a skirt, she thought, taking
an intense dislike to the green suede pants suit she
had chosen. But the bulky garments had seemed to
offer a means to disguise her painful thinness, and
Marsha had been enthusiastic when she had
presented herself to her.

But now, she was not so sure. Did she look too
severe—too angular? too *masculine* in clothes that
did nothing for her femininity? Even the russet silk
shirt she was wearing was plain and undramatic,
only its vivid colour suggesting a less consistent
attitude to style.

Whatever, it was too late now to change either
her mind or her clothes, and gathering all her
confidence, she made her presence known. But the
tentative tattoo was scarcely audible, and she was
obliged to knock again before evoking a reply.

'Hang on!' It was Ben's voice, and her heart
skipped a beat. 'I won't be a second.'

The few seconds he took before opening the
door seemed the longest of Shelley's life, and when
the door did move inward, she was almost
persuaded to take to her heels. What if he was still
angry with her? What if he refused to speak to her?
How would she cope with the blow it would deal
her after having her hopes lifted so high?

'*Shelley!*'

His expression of shock and amazement was not
encouraging, and it didn't help when he wrapped
the folds of a white bathrobe more closely about
him, with the air of someone wearing nothing
underneath. Evidently, he had been in either the

bath or the shower when she summoned him to the door, and although it should have put her at an advantage, it didn't.

Nevertheless, she was disturbed by the gauntness of his features. His illness—and what else?—had given his face a stark austerity, and even the pigment of his skin had faded to a pallid tan. The robe made it impossible to discern any other changes in his physical appearance, but she guessed that his skin was stretched tautly over his bones, and there was not an ounce of spare flesh on him.

'Hello, Ben,' she managed, squeezing her clutch bag tightly between her fingers. 'Can I speak to you?'

He hesitated, gripping the edge of the door and obstructing her passage. 'I thought you were my mother,' he said, obliquely. And then, his lips twisting in sudden comprehension, he added: 'Of course. She told you where I was. She must be more desperate than I thought.'

Shelley held up her head. 'Aren't you pleased to see me then?' she asked, half suspecting Marsha had not been completely truthful with her, and Ben expelled his breath wearily.

'That depends,' he said. 'If the only reason you've come here is to add your weight to my mother's argument that I shouldn't consider an overseas appointment, then no.'

Shelley quivered. 'And if it's not the only reason?'

Ben's mouth tightened. 'Then I should ask what other reason there could be,' he responded flatly. 'From what Berlitz told my mother, I gather you've succeeded in finding a new appointment, so it's not because you're out of a job. And if you've got some crazy notion that because you and my mother have apparently started speaking again we should resume our friendship, then forget it.'

Shelley caught her tongue between her teeth. 'Don't you want to be my friend, Ben?' she queried softly, and he scowled.

'No,' he replied succinctly. 'I don't want to be your friend. Now, do you mind if I terminate this conversation? As you can see, I was about to take a bath, and I'd like to get back to it before the water gets cold.'

Shelley took a deep breath. 'I'll wait.'

'No!'

'Yes.' Taking the biggest gamble of her life, Shelley brushed past him into his hotel room. 'I might even scrub your back if you ask me nicely.'

'Shelley——' There was a note of strain in his voice now, and she heard it with a sense of relief. Marsha had not been lying; Charles had not been lying; Ben was tearing himself to pieces, and it was all her fault.

'Close the door, Ben,' she said, knowing exactly what she must do, and although he swore, very colourfully, he did as he was asked.

'This isn't going to work, Shelley,' he got out harshly. 'I suppose my mother's told you that my engagement to Jennifer is all washed-up, and you feel a totally unnecessary sense of responsibility——'

'Stop talking such utter rot,' Shelley interrupted him huskily, placing her bag on top of his suitcase, and unbuttoning her jacket. Then, depositing it beside her bag, she sauntered casually across to the window. 'Not much of a view,' she remarked, noting the soot-smeared tower of a church across a paved square. 'But then, people don't usually come to hotels to look out of the window, do they? They're far more concerned with the reasons they're there.'

'Why are you here, Shelley?' asked Ben, at last,

and turning to find him pushing back his hair with weary fingers, she knew that for both of them there was no turning back.

'Would you believe—because I love you?' she asked, saying it lightly, forcing herself to be flippant, half afraid even now that she might have got it wrong, and Ben's breath escaped with a rush.

'How—how inconvenient for you,' he muttered, making no move towards her, and Shelley wondered tensely if they had actually gone too far.

'It's—only inconvenient if you want to make it so,' she ventured huskily, and Ben's lips curled.

'You mean—now that Jennifer's out of the way and my mother's apparently prepared to accept the fact of our relationship, you wouldn't object too strongly if we saw one another now and then?'

'No.' Shelley took a few steps towards him, and then came to a halt, deterred by his grim expression. 'No, that's not what I meant, Ben. I said I love you!'

'And what am I supposed to do about it?' he demanded. 'Stay in this country because if I go to Africa we'll have no chance to see one another?'

'No——'

'Or maybe you'd like me to find a post nearer London, hmm? In Buckinghamshire or Hertfordshire, perhaps. What about London itself? If that would make it easier for you.'

'Ben, stop it!'

'Why should I stop it? It's the truth, isn't it? You don't really care about me. One way or another, you and my mother have cooked up this plan to keep me on hand, like a lapdog, ready to perform, whenever the fancy takes you!'

'No——'

'Then what?' Ben uttered an ugly oath. 'You

can't mean anything more permanent. You've got a new job, remember? A position of some importance, isn't that the truth? and let's not forget I'm younger than you are, and far too naïve for my own good!'

'Oh, Ben.' Shelley shook her head. 'I know I've hurt you——'

'Like hell!'

'—but I hurt myself, too.'

'You?'

'Yes, me.' She narrowed the distance between them a little more, and spread her hands. 'Ben, the only reason I'm here is because I care about you. God knows, I didn't want to care about you. Like you say, I'm older, and I'm not the kind of woman you should want. When I went away, I thought I was doing the right thing—for you, for me, for everyone. I didn't believe you when you said you loved me. I wouldn't *let* myself believe you!'

'And now?' he enquired without emotion.

'Now?' She shook her head. 'That's up to you.'

'And your job?'

Ben's jaw was tight, as if he was having difficulty in maintaining his composure, and Shelley was encouraged.

'There is no job,' she told him, tentatively touching his sleeve. 'Oh—I've been offered one, but I haven't accepted it yet.'

'And are you going to?'

Shelley hesitated. 'That rather depends on you.'

Ben shook his head and turned away. 'I can't make your decisions for you.'

'I'm not asking you to.' Shelley stepped even closer, so that the hem of his bathrobe brushed her knees. 'But—you do still want me, don't you?'

Ben groaned, as if driven beyond his resistance, his hands groping unsteadily for her face, cradling it between his palms and stroking her lips with his. 'Yes, I want you,' he muttered, but there was no joy in the admission. 'But not on your terms,' he added, using his strength to propel her away. 'Now—will you get out of here?'

Shelley stared at him. 'What—terms?'

'I don't want an affair, Shelley,' he told her grimly, and the lines that bracketed his mouth gave him a maturity far beyond his years. 'You persuaded me once that it was enough, and I believed you. But it wasn't. I don't want to go through that again.'

'Oh, Ben!' Shelley trembled. 'Does that mean your offer is withdrawn?'

'What offer?'

Shelley held up her head. 'You asked me to marry you once,' she declared unsteadily. 'I didn't realise there was a limit to your proposal.'

'A limit?' Ben gazed at her as if he couldn't quite believe what he was hearing, and then, when comprehension dawned, he still continued to regard her with wary eyes. 'You don't—mean this.'

'Oh, yes, I do.' Shelley nodded vigorously, the action causing an upheaval in the securing of her hair, so that it fell about her shoulders in wild disorder. 'Oh——' She touched the recalcitrant strands with impatient fingers. 'Just when I wanted you to see me at my best.'

'Shelley!' His grated use of her name was accompanied by his hands, grasping her shoulders in a numbing grip. 'Shelley, if you're playing some game——'

'No game, darling,' she assured him, her hands going surely for the cord of his bathrobe. 'Mmm, that's much—much better—don't you think?'

*   *   *

An hour later Shelley regarded Ben teasingly across the mound of bubbles that filled the bath. And what a bath, she reflected ruefully. At least seven feet long and probably half as deep, with plenty of room for two people who didn't mind the intimacy. The whole bathroom was unique, a modern-gothic extravagance, with ultra-efficient plumbing and distinctly opulent, if slightly out-dated, fittings.

'Isn't this rather decadent?' she murmured mischieviously, leaning towards him. 'Much more comfortable than a shower. Do you think we could have a bath like this fitted in our house? I think I like the sensation of sitting between your legs.'

Ben's grin was rueful. 'I don't think my stamina would survive more than a few weeks,' he retorted, brushing her shoulder with his lips. 'Mmm, you know what's going to happen, don't you? And we're supposed to be meeting my mother for dinner at half-past-eight.'

'I'm sure she'll understand,' said Shelley huskily, abandoning her amusement as she met his hungry gaze. 'Oh, Ben, thank God you were strong enough for both of us! I couldn't have borne the thought of you married to someone else.'

The water lapped unheedingly over the side of the bath as Ben brought her alongside him, his mouth seeking her mouth as his hands sought other intimacies. 'I love you,' he told her simply, his urgent body hot against her stomach, and the explosion of their emotion left even Shelley feeling weak.

'Where do you want to live?' he asked her some time later, as they dried one another with the fluffy white towels. He hesitated. 'I suppose I could find a practice near London, if you want to accept that appointment.'

'I don't,' said Shelley honestly, looping her arms around his neck, delighting in their mutual nudity. 'As a matter of fact, I think I'd rather like to have children. And then your mother won't be thwarted in her desire to become a grandmother.'

'So long as I have you to myself for a while,' conceded Ben huskily. 'That's something I'm only just beginning to believe.'

'But you do believe it, don't you?' she insisted, pressing herself against him, and his eagerly stirring body was all the answer she needed.

'So,' he said emotively, 'and what if I suggested going back to Low Burton? Frank Chater would be delighted. He didn't want me to leave.'

'Not even——'

'No. Not even in spite of Jennifer,' finished Ben softly. 'I think Frank realised some time ago that we weren't exactly made for one another. But Mrs Chater makes it virtually impossible for him to voice an opinion.' He gave a wry smile. 'You know what they say—look at the mother and you'll see the daughter twenty years on!'

Shelley bit her lip. 'But will it matter to you—in your work, I mean—your marrying someone else and continuing to live in Low Burton?'

'I doubt it.' Ben was philosophical. 'What's more to the point—will you be able to stand it?'

Shelley snuggled closer. 'Well, I was born in the dales, you know,' she reminded him smugly. 'And so long as we're together, I suspect it won't be so bad!'

Here's how to get this special offer from Harlequin!

As simple as 1...2...3!

1. Each month, save one Treasury Edition coupon from your favorite Romance or Presents novel.
2. In four months you'll have saved four Treasury Edition coupons (<u>only one coupon per month allowed</u>).
3. Then all you have to do is fill out and return the order form provided, along with the four Treasury Edition coupons required and $1.00 for postage and handling.

Mail to: Harlequin Reader Service

RT1-E-2

In the U.S.A.
2504 West Southern Ave.
Tempe, AZ 85282

In Canada
P.O. Box 2800, Postal Station A
5170 Yonge Street
Willowdale, Ont. M2N 6J3

Please send me my FREE copy of the Janet Dailey Treasury Edition. I have enclosed the four Treasury Edition coupons required and $1.00 for postage and handling along with this order form.

(Please Print)

NAME _____

ADDRESS _____

CITY _____

STATE/PROV. _____ ZIP/POSTAL CODE _____

SIGNATURE _____

This offer is limited to one order per household.

SUPPLIES LIMITED

This special Janet Dailey offer expires January 1986.

Take 4 best-selling love stories FREE
Plus get a FREE surprise gift!